MW01170198

LONG RIDE TO BUFFALO

ALSO BY ROBERT VAUGHAN

The Tenderfoot

On the Oregon Trail

Cold Revenge

Iron Horse

Outlaw Justice

Western Fiction Ten Pack

Orphan Cowboy

Slaughter at Rebel Ridge

Reckoning Day

Trail to Brimstone

Hidden Hero

Outpost in the Desert

The Founders Series

The Western Adventures of Cade McCall

Faraday Series

Lucas Cain Series

Chaney Brothers Westerns

Arrow and Saber Series

The Crocketts Series

Remington Series

...and many more

LONG RIDE TO BUFFALO

ROBERT VAUGHAN

WOLFPACK
PUBLISHING
— EST 2013 —

Long Ride to Buffalo
Paperback Edition
Copyright © 2025 by Robert Vaughan

Wolfpack Publishing
1707 E. Diana Street
Tampa, FL 33609

www.wolfpackpublishing.com

All rights reserved. No part of this book may be reproduced in any form or by any electronic or mechanical means, including information storage and retrieval systems, without express written permission from the publisher, except for the use of brief quotations in reviews. Any use of this publication to train generative artificial intelligence (AI) technologies is expressly prohibited.

This book is a work of fiction. References to historical events, real people, or real places are used fictitiously. Any similarity to real persons, living or dead, is purely coincidental and not intended by the author.

All brand names and product names used in this book are trademarks, registered trademarks, or trade names of their respective holders. Wolfpack Publishing is not associated with any product or vendor in this book.

Paperback ISBN 979-8-89567-193-1
Ebook ISBN 979-8-89567-192-4
LCCN 2024951390

LONG RIDE TO BUFFALO

PROLOGUE

I t was an early afternoon in the middle of May 1886, and Theresa, Wyoming, was a busy little town. Wagons were parked in front of the business establishments lining both sides of the one long street, while the board sidewalks were crowded with men and women looking in shop windows or hurrying to and fro, attending to whatever it was that had drawn them into town that day.

Five men rode in from the south end of town onto that commercial scene, and a few of the passersby glanced at the leader, a medium-sized man with a cadaverous face, a full, sweeping mustache, and dark, piercing eyes. Brody Pike and his fellow riders surveyed the town carefully, studying the rooflines of the false-fronted buildings, looking into the open doorways, and peering down the alleyways. The outlaws, who were wanted all over Wyoming Territory, entered any town the same careful way, knowing at any given time they might well ride into an ambush of lawmen, vigilantes, or just good citizens.

"What the hell? Is this Saturday?" Jasper Maddox asked, scratching his dark stubby beard.

"How am I supposed to know?" Pike replied, pulling the brim of his Stetson down tighter on his head. "I don't keep no damn calendar."

"Seems to me like there's just too many people here," Maddox observed.

"Maybe that's to the good. The more people in the street, the easier it'll be for us to get away," Pike responded.

"There! There's the bank right down there on the corner, just like I said," one of the other men, Rafe Dempsey, pointed out. He nodded so vigorously that his stovepipe hat almost fell off his head.

"How much money you reckon's in it, Pike?" Slim Hawkins asked, his cold blue eyes lighting up with greed.

"I don't know. Maybe a couple of thousand dollars. Maybe more. It don't make no difference. A bank's a bank, and money's money."

"How are we goin' to do this? We just goin' to ride right in and hit it, or what?"

"Not so fast," Pike answered. He pointed to a small restaurant across the street from the bank. "What say we get us somethin' to eat first? From there, we can check out the street. You know. See what kind of action is goin' on around here."

"Yeah, something to eat. That's a good idea," Maddox agreed.

"Maddox, anytime we eat, it's a good idea as far as

you're concerned," Jim Porter quipped, tugging on his light-brown mustache and the rest of the men laughed.

"Well, I tell you, Porter, I ain't seen you turn down too many meals yourself," Maddox countered, and the men laughed again.

Tying their horses in front of the restaurant, the riders went inside and ordered ham, eggs, biscuits, and fried potatoes. Their food came, and to anyone watching who had not seen their faces adorning wanted posters, they appeared merely to be five friends lingering over a meal for some friendly conversation.

Shortly after two o'clock, the five men left the restaurant. Porter and Maddox then rode to the north end of town and Slim trotted to the south end, while Pike and Dempsey casually walked their horses across the street and hitched them directly in front of the bank. For a few minutes they stood at the door; then, suddenly, the other three men came riding back from either end of town at a full gallop, shooting and whooping loudly, and scattering the terrified bystanders. With the citizens' attention diverted from the bank, Pike and Dempsey smiled at each other and rushed into the bank.

"Put your hands up!" the outlaw leader shouted gruffly the moment they stepped inside.

The two women customers screamed, while one male customer shouted out in anger, only to be clubbed down by the butt of Dempsey's pistol.

"Everyone keep quiet in here," Dempsey commanded. "We'll do all the talkin'."

"You," Pike ordered the bank teller nearest the vault, "start emptyin' out that safe."

The middle-aged bank teller put his hand on the door but then, to Pike's surprise, abruptly slammed it shut.

"That didn't do you no good," Pike snarled. "You're just gonna have to open it again."

"I can't," the teller replied, a self-satisfied look on his moon-shaped face. "It has a time lock."

"A time lock? What the hell does that mean?"

"It means it's impossible for anyone to open it until eight o'clock tomorrow morning," the teller said. He smiled triumphantly. "This is one bank you won't be robbing today, Mr. Brody Pike."

"Damn your hide!" Pike growled angrily. Aiming his revolver at the defiant teller, he pulled the trigger and shot the man in the chest.

Eyes widening, the teller gasped, fell against the front of the vault, and then slid down to a sitting position. Within a few seconds he was dead.

"Empty the cash drawer and let's get the hell out of here," Pike ordered, and Dempsey began scooping the loose bills into a sack.

A young office boy, unnoticed by either Pike or Dempsey, managed to crawl through the back room and out the back door. Once clear of the bank, he ran through the alley out to the main street, shouting, "The bank is being robbed! The bank is being robbed!"

The townspeople suddenly recognized the great show of gunplay for the ruse it was and began arming themselves. Ducking behind barrels and crates, men started firing at the three mounted outlaws. They immediately began firing back, and Jasper Maddox felled one man as he rose up from behind a crate to get off a shot from his rifle. The man screamed and clutched his shoulder, then fell behind his cover.

Turning their horses to and fro, making themselves moving targets and therefore harder to hit, Maddox, Porter, and Hawkins waited with obvious impatience for their cohorts to emerge from the bank. They fired off shot after shot, keeping the townsmen busy protecting their own lives. Occasionally one of the defenders got off a shot of his own, but no bullets struck any of the outlaws.

Pike and Dempsey rushed out the front door of the bank, with the gang leader holding the money sack in one hand and his revolver in the other. They stopped in their tracks at the sight of the battle taking place twenty yards down the street.

"Damn it, Pike, I knew that was too much shootin' goin' on to just be our boys!" Dempsey shouted over the din.

Seeing the men come out of the bank, the citizens of Theresa swarmed to the building, ready for them. "Hold it! You ain't goin' nowhere!" a middle-aged townsman called, a deep frown on his pudgy face. At almost the same time he yelled, he fired his revolver. His bullet missed the outlaws and punched through the front window of the bank. Another man then fired a shot, and his bullet went through Rafe Dempsey's top hat.

"Let's go, let's go!" Pike yelled, shooting back as they ran toward their horses.

From the restaurant in which the men had eaten a

few minutes earlier, a citizen, food stains spattered on the front of his shirt, appeared with a shotgun. He let go a blast, but the gun was loaded only with a light bird shot, and his pellets merely peppered the outlaws without penetrating their skin. Another man with a shotgun fired, and the other front window of the bank came crashing down.

A man then killed Jim Porter's horse, but the outlaw merely leaped out of the saddle, leaving his dead animal in the dirt, and ran toward the nearest hitch rail. The many horses left tied by their owners all along the street were spooked by all the gunfire, and they reared and pulled against their restraints.

Porter grabbed the one nearest him and swung into the saddle as the horse's owner started forward in protest, shouting, "That's my horse!"

"You won't be needin' it no more," Porter retorted, shooting the man between the eyes from nearly point-blank range. The bullet came out the back of the man's skull and embedded itself in the dusty street just before the man flopped onto the same spot, his unseeing eyes open in surprise.

With all of them now mounted, the robbers galloped toward the south end of town, but in an attempt to stop them, several men rolled a wagon out into the middle of the dusty street and tipped it over, barricading the way. They then gathered behind it, rifles held at the ready.

"What the hell? What do we do now, Pike?" Slim Hawkins yelled.

"This way!" Pike shouted back, and he reined his mount around, spinning it toward the large plate-glass window fronting a dressmaking shop. He urged his horse forward, and the animal leaped through the window, shattering the glass with an enormous crashing sound and clearing the way for the other four horses that followed close behind.

There were a number of women in the shop, including one being fitted for a new dress. Covering her corseted body with her arms, she and the other ladies screamed in terror as they made a mad dash to get out of the way. The horses clattered and skidded across the wooden floor, then ran through the back door and into an open field behind the store. It was a brilliant move on Pike's part, for none of the towns-people were yet mounted, and by the time they had reached their horses and come around the edge of town, the bank robbers had completely disappeared into the timbered hills.

Brody Pike, Wyoming's most wanted outlaw, had struck again.

ONE

Although it was late at night, the campfire still burned brightly, casting its glow over Brody Pike and the four members of his gang, who were gathered around it, basking in its warmth. They were finally eating their meager supper of beans and coffee, the rich aroma of which permeated the air.

The men were not dressed in standard trail gear. In fact, they were dressed in no particular way that would classify them or identify them as belonging to a certain occupation, for they had chosen their clothes on availability rather than style. Pike, at forty-one, the oldest of the group, wore a gray, misshapen Stetson stained with sweat and oil from his lank dark hair. Over his red flannel shirt and denim trousers he wore a brown tweed jacket that seemed more appropriate to a fireplace than the campfire he was staring at angrily with his piercing dark eyes.

Rafe Dempsey's trousers had once belonged to a

gentleman's formal evening ensemble—which did not mean that Dempsey was a gentleman or that he himself had ever dressed so elegantly—only that he had bought the trousers for ten cents at a secondhand clothing stoie. He had also bought, and was presently wearing, a stovepipe hat, having admired the one Abraham Lincoln had worn in photographs he had seen.

Slim Hawkins wore a brightly colored Mexican serape, not as a mark of his heritage, but for the warmth it provided. Jim Porter, who had deserted the Army some three years earlier, still wore the blue trousers of a cavalry trooper, and the hat on his head was an old Army-issue kepi. Jasper Maddox was the only one wearing clothes appropriate to the situation —a buckskin jacket, denim trousers, and a green plaid shirt.

However, though the men were dressed in a hodgepodge of clothes, they were unified by several elements—all wore guns, all were rough and hard-looking, they seldom shaved, and they bathed even more rarely.

"How much money did we get from that bank back there?" Porter asked.

"I ain't counted it exactly," Pike answered, lifting a spoonful of beans to this mouth, then eating noisily. "Dempsey, you was the one scooped it into the sack. What would you make it to be?"

"Not as much as it could've been," Dempsey grumbled, drumming his spoon angrily on the side of his tin plate. "What really makes me mad is that teller closin' the vault door like he did. Who'd a thought a bank in a two-bit town like Theresa'd have a time lock! No tellin' how much money was in that safe." He shook his head. "Little bastard deserved that bullet Brody put in his chest. I don't reckon we got any more than five hundred dollars from the cash drawer."

"Five hundred?" Slim yelped. "You mean to tell me we had a shoot-out with half the town, killed a few of 'em, and it was all for no more'n five hundred dollars?"

"That's about the size of it," Pike snapped.

Dempsey took off his top hat, then held it out for the others to contemplate. "Who'd of thought the whole town'd fight so damn hard over five hundred measly dollars?" he asked. He put his hand up inside the high crown of the hat, then stuck a finger through the hole and wriggled it at the others. "Lookee here, I damn near got my head blowed off—and for what? My share don't hardly come to a hundred dollars."

"Sometimes folks fight hardest when they ain't got much to protect," the gang leader muttered. His dark eyes glowed red in the reflected light as he looked at his cohort and then gestured with his spoon at the man's unfinished pan of food. "Hey, Dempsey, you gonna eat them beans or not?"

"You wanna know the truth of it, Pike, I'm getting' damn sick of beans," Dempsey replied, handing his plate over to Pike, who scraped the beans off into his own plate.

Pouring himself a cup of coffee, Slim Hawkins hunkered down into his serape and remarked, "Yeah, Pike, I ain't complainin' man, but the next time we hold us up a bank, let's make sure it ain't got one of them time lock safes in it, all right?"

"Have a little patience, Slim. This job was just to get us a little operatin' money is all," Pike replied, a smug expression on his face. "Truth is, I got us a deal planned now that's gonna bring us enough money so's we can quit if we want to." His eyes gleaming, he paused for effect and then asked, "How does a hundred thousand dollars to divvy up sound to you boys?"

"A hundred thousand dollars?" Slim shouted. "Whooee, I didn't even know there was that much money in the world!" He tugged thoughtfully on his dark mustache and then asked, "Where're we gonna find that kind of money?"

"Remember when I told all you boys that I was gonna make you rich one day?" Pike queried. "Well, that day's near to hand."

"One hundred thousand or five hundred dollars— what difference does it make if a man has to hide out in the mountains all the time and eat nothin' but beans?" Dempsey complained, tossing his empty plate onto the ground.

"Dempsey, you'd bitch if you were hung with a new rope." Porter snickered, and they all laughed.

"I reckon we'll find out the truth of that someday," Slim observed, "seein' as we're all probably gonna end up doin' a little dance for the hangman."

"I'd rather be hung than spend any more time in prison," Brody Pike rejoined. "There's some things worse than dyin', and bein' in prison is one of 'em."

Unknown to the band of outlaws, they were being

observed and overheard. Just beyond the circle of fire-light, Clay Donovan was sneaking among the boulders that half ringed the campsite, being careful not to make any noise.

Tall, lean, and muscular, Clay was only twenty-six, but he had seen his share of hard times, and his hand-some face and clear blue eyes reflected a maturity beyond his years. His sandy hair was matted with sweat, and he sported a four-day stubble—not because he was growing a beard, but because it had been that long since he had had the opportunity to shave. Like the men in the camp, Clay Donovan was armed and rawhide-tough. Unlike them, however, he had a sense of values and knew right from wrong—and he was there now because he intended to correct a wrong.

Although it was the middle of May, spring came late to Wyoming's Rattlesnake Mountain Range, and that night was particularly cold. Clay was wearing only a cotton shirt, having left his long, tan duster rolled up on the back of his saddle for fear of tripping on it. He shivered as he envied the fire that Brody Pike and his men were enjoying and blew on the palms of his hands in a futile effort to warm them.

Having moved down closer, hiding behind a large boulder, he had been able to hear what was being said in the camp, and he had to agree with the last comment. Being in prison was worse than dying... which was why he had been willing to risk his life a few days ago in order to escape from the territorial prison.

Never, even in his most terrible nightmare, had Clay Donovan expected to wind up in jail, but that was exactly where he had spent the last two years, after being framed by the very man he was staring at —Brody Pike—and had also killed his brother, Vince. Clay thought about those two years in prison—the dehumanization, the awful food, and especially the abandoned hopes and lost souls of those who were in there with him, and as he circled the campsite, he recalled all too vividly the events leading up to his imprisonment.

He and his older brother had been building a ranch and working hard to fulfill their shared dream. In order to help make ends meet until the ranch became self-supporting, Clay had taken on an extra job. While Vince stayed home and tended the ranch, Clay drove a stagecoach for the Wyoming Express Company.

Clay had heard of Brody Pike—as had just about everyone else in Wyoming Territory. Pike and his gang of cutthroats had moved across the countryside like a prairie fire, leaving a string of murders and robberies in their wake. But Clay was not a lawman, so Brody Pike barely occupied his thoughts.

However, that was all to change.

Shortly after Clay had completed what was to be his last stagecoach run, he had hurried home to the ranch to help his brother with the spring roundup of cattle. It had been a good winter, with very few losses to wolves or weather, and a number of calves had been born. At long last it looked as if the two brothers were about to turn the ranch into a profitable operation, which meant Clay could give up his stagecoach job and spend full time on the ranch. And it also meant that Vince would be able to ask the daughter of a neighboring rancher to marry him.

There was no such girl on the horizon for Clay. Though he had never said anything—and never would because his older brother had staked the claim first—Clay did not think he could ever be interested in a woman unless he could find one exactly like Vince's girl. She was beautiful and high-spirited, and she knew horses and cattle as well as any man. Clay thought that she was perfect and would be the perfect rancher's wife. Unfortunately that rancher would be Vince, not he.

For two days, the brothers had searched all the draws and canyons of their ranch, making certain that they rounded up every last calf for branding. After they had finished, Clay and Vince decided to go into town for a little relaxation in celebration of their newfound status as "gentlemen" ranchers.

"Well, ranchers anyway," Vince had agreed, a broad grin splitting his ruggedly handsome face. "I'm not all that certain about the gentleman part."

"That's the part that I *am* sure about," Clay had retorted. "Ma taught us to be gentlemen—she never taught us to be ranchers."

"Maybe Pa would have," Vince had mused.

"I often wonder what he was like. Do you remember him, Vince?" the younger brother had queried.

"I can remember him coming home once during

the war," Vince had answered, a sad smile on his face. "I remember his sword...I thought it was the most wonderful thing I had ever seen. He let me hold it. I must've killed a hundred Rebels with it—at least, in my imagination."

"I don't remember any of that."

His older brother had softly replied, "No way you could. You were only two years old when Pa was killed at Shiloh. I was six."

They had continued on toward town when suddenly Clay's horse threw a shoe, and the two men had been forced to stop. Vince had affectionately scolded, "I told you the day before yesterday that that shoe looked loose. Some rancher you are, little brother. You can't even keep your horse shod." Grinning, he had continued. "Never mind. I've got some tools in my saddlebag. Get down from there and we'll take care of it."

The brothers had no sooner gotten off their horses to look at the problem when five men had come galloping hard over the ridge. The man in the lead had pointed at them and then headed directly toward the young ranchers.

As the riders reined to an abrupt halt, Vince had greeted, "Howdy."

"Havin' some trouble?" one of the riders—a man with a long, deeply hollowed face and a large handlebar mustache—had asked, swinging down from his horse. The man's four friends had then dismounted as well.

"Nothing serious," Vince had replied lightly. "Just a loose shoe is all." He had squinted at the men.

"Don't believe I ever met any of you gents. You just come into the territory?"

"Yeah, we're lookin' for work."

Vince had shrugged. "I'm afraid you're too late. Spring roundup's over, so I doubt there's much work around any of the ranches right now. Maybe you fellas can find something in one of the towns—at a livery or stage line, perhaps."

Nodding, Clay had suggested, "Matter of fact, the stage line in Buffalo is looking for a hostler."

"Where's this Buffalo?"

"Just north of here, maybe five or six miles," Vince had answered. "We're going there now to have a couple of beers. You're welcome to ride along with us." He then laughed. "That is, if my brother ever gets that shoe fixed."

Ignoring his brother's jibe, the younger rancher had lifted the horse's foot and then leaned over to examine the hoof more closely. Suddenly Vince had yelled, "What the hell?" Clay had looked up just as one of the riders slammed the butt of his pistol down on Clay's head. At the same time that he had felt a sharp stab of pain, Clay also thought he heard a loud popping noise, but then everything went black.

"Get up," someone had demanded.

Opening his eyes, Clay had found that he was lying on his stomach, with his face in the dirt. He had no idea where he was or why he was lying on the ground, though he sensed there were several people standing around, looking down at him.

His head throbbed and his brain seemed to be

shrouded in fog. Who were they, and why were they there? Why was *he* there?

The young rancher had tried to get up, but everything started spinning so badly that he nearly passed out again. He was conscious of a terrible pain on the top of his head, and when he had reached up and touched the spot gingerly, his fingers came away sticky with blood. Holding his fingers in front of his eyes, he had stared at them in surprise.

"What happened?" he had finally asked, his tongue thick, as though he had been drinking too much.

"There was a fallin' out among thieves, that's what happened," came a gruff voice. "The other boys turned on you two, emptied your bank sacks, and took the money with 'em."

Utterly confused, Clay had muttered, "I don't know what you're talking about."

"No sense in tryin' to get away with that line of bull," the man had said. "You're the one we want, all right. And just 'cause you wound up without any of the money, it don't make you no less guilty. You're gonna hang, fella. Your partner would hang too, if your friends hadn't already killed him. Now, are you gonna get up, or am I gonna have to tie a rope around your feet and drag you all the way back to Banner?"

"Who are you?" Clay had asked, managing to make it to his knees and looking up. He had been right in sensing that there were several people around him. In addition to the one who was obviously in charge—a burly man of about forty-five with a deeply lined face —there were six more men glaring at him and brandishing an arsenal of weapons ranging from revolvers to rifles to shotguns—all of which were pointing at him.

"I'm the town marshal from Banner," the burly man had answered, holding open his jacket to expose the tin star pinned to his shirt, "and these here men are my deputies. I reckon you and your friends figured you could rob our bank 'cause we're so small, but you got yourselves another think comin'. Get up."

"I don't know what you're talking about," Clay had repeated and started to get to his feet when he suddenly noticed his brother. Vince was lying on his back, his arms flopped out on either side of him.

"Vince!" he screamed. "Oh, my god!" Seeing the ugly black hole between his brother's eyes, Clay had hurried to him. He had put his hand on Vince's neck to check for a pulse, but before he even touched him, he had known his brother was dead. Clay had instantly felt a profound sense of sorrow and loneliness.

"Is that this fella's name? Vince?"

"Yes. Vince Donovan," Clay had choked out. "He's my brother. I'm Clay Donovan."

"Well, Clay Donovan, I'm arrestin' you for the murderin' and bank robbin' you and the others done up in Banner," the marshal had announced. One of the other men had grabbed Clay roughly, twisted his hands behind his back and then shackled them together.

"Help him on his horse," the marshal had ordered. "And then pick up them empty bank bags. We'll be needin' 'em as evidence."

Roughly put onto his horse, Clay Donovan had protested, "Marshal, please listen to me! My brother and I didn't hold up any bank! We've been working on our ranch for the last two weeks! We were just heading into Buffalo to celebrate finishing our spring roundup when we were jumped by five men!"

"Uh huh," the lawman had answered, unimpressed. "You got any witnesses can verify any of this tale?"

"Well, no," Clay had admitted. "We've been out on the range, and we don't have any hands. There are... *were* just the two of us."

"Too bad you ain't got no witnesses, Donovan, 'cause I do. At least half a dozen of 'em. And they'll every one of 'em swear they seen you and your brother ridin' out of town with Brody Pike."

Clay's eyes had widened with surprise as he suddenly realized who the five riders were. "Brody Pike? Well, I'll be damned. *That's* who that was!" Shaking his head angrily, the young rancher had insisted. "Well, your witnesses are wrong—dead wrong!"

"Mister, *I'm* one of them witnesses," the marshal had rejoined emphatically, pointing to his chest. "So don't you go tellin' me what I did and what I didn't see." He then pointed at Clay's chest, adding, "I remember them plaid shirts you and your brother's wearin' like as if there was a picture of 'em drawn on my eyeballs."

Bewildered, Clay had glanced down at the shirt he wore, then at the shirt his brother was wearing, and he had wondered if he was going mad. They were not the shirts they had put on when they had left the ranch! Gasping sharply, he had then remembered that two of Pike's cohorts had been wearing shirts just like these.

Squeezing his eyes shut, then opening them, as if somehow that would bring things into focus, Clay had reconstructed a picture of what had happened. Apparently Brody Pike had used Clay and Vince to buy some time from the posse that had given chase after the bank robbery. They had knocked out Clay, killed Vince and then changed shirts with them. To enhance the frame, they had even left a couple of empty bank sacks.

"Marshal, you're making a big mistake!" Clay had desperately declared.

"No, friend," the lawman had responded. "The only ones who made any mistakes around here was you and your brother. And you boys made three of 'em." Ticking them off on his fingers, he had enumerated: "Your first one was in pickin' a bank in my town to rob, your second was in trustin' a man like Brody Pike—you can see where that got you—and your third was in getting' yourself caught. Now, let's go."

"What about my brother? You aren't just going to leave him here?"

"I'll send word to the undertaker in Buffalo to come out and get him." Smirking, he had added, "Don't worry. He ain't goin' nowhere."

Clay had not even been allowed to attend his brother's burial. At the time of the funeral, the young rancher was attending his own trial. Officials of the Wyoming Express Company as well as Sheriff Seth Reardon of Buffalo had testified on Clay's behalf, but the case hinged on the accounts of the six eyewitnesses, all good citizens of Banner...and Banner was where the trial was held.

Other than the "good character" testimony provided by his friends, Clay had had absolutely no defense. The only thing that had saved him from hanging was the testimony of several of the witnesses who believed the bullet that killed the deputy had been fired by Brody Pike himself. Clay had been found innocent of murder but guilty of armed robbery, and he was sentenced to twenty years of hard labor in the territorial prison.

Clay Donovan had been a model prisoner for two years. Then, a week ago, a lawyer had ridden to the prison to talk to his client. After tying his horse outside the warden's office, the visitor had checked his pistol with the warden's clerk and hung his hat and the long tan duster he had worn for the ride from Buffalo on a coat rack in the warden's office. The young prisoner, who had been mopping the office floor, had watched it all.

Minutes later, purely by happenstance, a fight had broken out among some of the prisoners. From all over the prison, guards had rushed to the scene to break it up before it spread into a riot. The warden and his clerk had also hurried out into the yard, and the lawyer had followed along, just to watch the action.

Seeing that the lawyer's horse, gun, duster, and hat were unattended, Clay had quickly put the mop down, strapped on the gun, slipped into the duster, pulled the hat low over his face and then mounted the lawyer's horse and ridden out the front gate just as if he had had every right to do so. The guards at the gate had been so busy looking back toward the yard at all the excitement that they had barely glanced at Clay as he rode out.

———

It was pure luck rather than good tracking skills that had brought Clay Donovan to Brody Pike's campsite. Traveling by night so as to avoid any posse that might be out looking for him, Clay had seen the glow of Pike's campfire and cautiously approached. He had been expecting to find some cowboys in the middle of a roundup bedded down for the night, not the notorious outlaw and his gang discussing their last robbery and planning their next.

Now that he had found Pike, he was not exactly certain what he was going to do with him. There had been a time, during his first five or six months in prison, when he had been so filled with rage, all he could think of was avenging his brother's death—but now what he wanted was to prove his innocence. He was not sure how capturing Brody Pike would do that —his idea was vaguely formed at best—but he felt that if he could capture him and turn him over to the authorities, he could force the outlaw to clear him.

Deciding to try to improve his position to get the drop on the gang, Clay moved down through the boulders. Suddenly his foot dislodged a large rock, and it tumbled down noisily.

"What the hell was that?" Brody Pike yelled, his pan of beans flying as he stood up quickly, his gun in his hand in an instant. "Dempsey, douse them flames!" he ordered. Coffee was immediately thrown on the fire, and it sizzled and smoked as it went out.

Fearing discovery, Clay started to scramble over the boulder-strewn ground to where he had left his horse.

"There, I saw something!" someone shouted, and the shout was followed almost immediately by a shot.

The others began firing as well, and as they fired, the flames from the muzzles of their guns lit up the dark like flashes of summer lightning. Bullets sparked off the boulders all around Clay, and one ricocheted so close to his ear that he could feel the sharp puff of air at its passing. It ran through his mind that he suddenly knew how his father must have felt during the war, with enemy fire striking all around him. He only hoped he would not end up the same way—dead with a bullet in his skull.

"After him!" one of the bandits shouted.

Another shot was fired, and it hit a rock by Clay's feet, digging out a piece of rock and slamming it painfully into the young prisoner's leg. He was thankful for the thick, sturdy denim cloth that protected his skin; otherwise, the shard would have penetrated as though it were a slug.

He neared the place where he had left his horse when another slug whizzed by his head. Reflexively leaping to one side, the ground where he had been standing a moment before was suddenly struck by a bullet, and a piece of sod went flying into the air.

Running nimbly, having occasionally to fling himself flat on the ground, Clay finally made it to his horse. Not until he was mounted did he send a shot back toward his pursuers, using the flame bursts from their guns as targets. He then urged the horse forward, but it was the mount he had stolen from the lawyer, and the lawyer had obviously selected it for gentleness and ease of handling, not for its agility and quickness. If he had been riding a responsive quarter horse, he might have escaped into the darkness. Instead, the horse, already frightened by the gunshots and by demands being made of him, balked, and then refused to make a jump.

Clay was panicky. He could tell by their voices, getting steadily and increasingly louder, that the outlaws were drawing closer, and they kept up their barrage of shots as they approached. Suddenly the young prisoner felt, rather than heard, a bullet hit his horse. The animal shuddered once and then went down. Leaping quickly from the saddle to keep from being pinned underneath, Clay hit the ground painfully, crying out as he fell.

With a shout of triumph, believing they had him, his pursuers pressed forward, but Clay rolled on the ground, trying to keep his visibility to a minimum. Suddenly the ground gave way as he came to the edge of a steep cliff that was barely evident in the light of the cloud-covered moon, and he cautiously started descending. Finding purchase for his hands and feet wherever he could—in crevices, scrub trees, and brush —he worked his way down and soon reached the bottom, some one hundred feet below. The moon came out from behind a cloud for a moment, and Clay discerned a well-used animal trail and started running. Within minutes, he could no longer hear Brody Pike or his men.

He kept going for another quarter hour. Finally, assuming he was safe, the exhausted young man crawled into the middle of a thick stand of bushes and then curled up and went to sleep.

When dawn broke a few hours later, Clay Donovan took stock of his situation. He had managed to escape the outlaw band, but all of his gear was back with his fallen horse. He had nothing—not even a canteen—and now not only was he wanted by the law, but he was in the middle of nowhere and had lost all track of his quarry.

With a sigh, he stood and began the long trek down from the mountains.

———

Rebecca McBride opened her eyes and looked through the window of the railroad car and then smiled with pleasure. The dawn sky was streaked with various shades of red, gold, and purple, and she had almost forgotten how wonderful the sunrises and sunsets could be in Wyoming. Toying with a lock of her long dark hair, she lay in her berth listening to the rhythmic clack the wheels made on the tracks and enjoying the patterns and colors of the breathtakingly beautiful, ever-changing sky.

No! Rebecca suddenly reprimanded herself, her light-blue eyes flashing and her fair skin flushing. *I won't enjoy this!* Angrily turning her head away from the window, she stared at the heavy green curtain that covered her berth. She refused to allow herself to be seduced by the rugged beauty of this land, for she knew that this country had little to offer other than brutal winters, blistering summers, hard work, and heartbreak.

Rebecca reminded herself of the cruel tricks Wyoming had already played on her. Two years ago she had suffered a personal tragedy so traumatic that her father had sent her away to a woman's school in Boston. At the time, she had not wanted to go, but her father had insisted, and the experience had turned into an awakening for Rebecca.

The school she had attended was in the forefront of women's education, and she had come to regard herself in an entirely new light. Additionally, she got a glimpse of a world that she had not even known existed: She discovered great libraries that contained more books than she could read in a hundred lifetimes; she visited museums to view some of the world's greatest art treasures; she attended concerts where the music was so beautiful it could rival the Heavenly Hosts; she saw plays and ballets performed by the foremost artists of the day; and she attended lectures given by the most learned men in the world.

Boston had indoor plumbing and gas lights, steam heat and elevators, hospitals where medical miracles were being performed, and even telephones. After two years, Rebecca had come to believe that Boston was the only place to be, and she wondered why anyone would ever want to live in a place like Wyoming.

Then she had received a letter from her father explaining that a very difficult winter had dealt the ranch such serious financial setbacks that he could no longer afford to keep her in the school. Stoically, Rebecca looked upon that as but one more of the penalties Wyoming extracted from those people crazy enough or stubborn enough to choose to live there.

In the letter, Rebecca's father asked her to please come back home, and this Rebecca was doing. But in her own mind she was going home only long enough to convince her father to sell his ranch and return East with her. In Boston, her father could live quite comfortably for the rest of his life just on the money he could get from selling the ranch.

On the other side of the heavy green curtain that covered her berth and afforded her some privacy, Rebecca heard the porter walking through the cars, announcing that breakfast was now being served in the dining car. With a deep sigh, she roused herself and struggled into her clothes; then she climbed down from the berth and hurried to the end of the car to the washroom.

"Ah, dear, there you are!" Kate Langston, a smile lighting up her strikingly lovely face, greeted Rebecca as she arrived in the dining car a few minutes later. The sunlight streaming through the window glinted on Kate's auburn hair, making it look like burnished copper. Kate's eight-year-old son, Tad, hurried around to pull the chair out for Rebecca as she joined her friends.

"Thank you, Tad. What a wonderful young gentleman you are," Rebecca enthused as she gathered the long skirt of her green silk frock around her to sit.

"Today's the day, Miss McBride," Tad remarked, ignoring the compliment. "We get home today!"

"Not quite, Tad," Kate reminded her son. "Remember, we still have quite a long stagecoach ride ahead of us."

"Yes, but at least we're in Wyoming," Tad countered. "I'm really glad to be back. I hated Philadelphia."

Rebecca laughed and shook her head. "So here are the two of us. You can hardly wait to get back, and I wish I didn't have to return."

Coincidentally, Rebecca had run across Kate and her son as they were changing trains in Omaha. Before she had left Wyoming, Rebecca had known the Langstons, for Kate and her husband had run a small hotel and restaurant in Buffalo, Wyoming, which was the town nearest her father's ranch. Then Kate's husband died last year, and her sister, who lived in Philadelphia, insisted that Kate and Tad come to live with her and her husband. Closing up her hotel, Kate had rented out the lobby to the Wyoming Express Company to use as their depot. Then she had packed up her clothes and some personal belongings and took her son East.

It had not worked out. Kate missed having her own home, and she missed her friends. But most of all, she missed Wyoming. Finally, when she could no longer resist the desire to return, she said a tearful farewell to her sister and bought train tickets back to Wyoming.

When Kate and Rebecca had met on the train in Omaha, they immediately renewed their friendship.

They proved to be wonderful company for one another during the long train ride, even though there was quite a difference in age between the two women, for Rebecca was in her early twenties while Kate was in her midthirties. The physical differences between them were equally as great—the one brunette and dark complexioned and the other redheaded and fair —though each woman was exceptionally lovely in her own way.

The two women chatted cheerily through breakfast; then Rebecca noticed that the boy had eaten very little. "Tad, I don't believe it," the young brunette joshed. "You, the world's champion pancake eater, are passing up your last morning's stack of them?"

"I guess I'm just not very hungry, Miss McBride," Tad answered.

Kate put a solicitous hand on her son's forehead. "I don't know, Rebecca, he was complaining of a stomachache during the night," she explained. "It may have been something he ate."

"Yes, or perhaps it's train sickness," Rebecca suggested. "I've observed that it can sometimes occur even if you've been riding for several days with no previous ill effects."

"Yes," Kate agreed, nodding, "perhaps so." She smiled. "If that's what it is, he'll certainly have the opportunity to recover soon enough. The conductor told me a short while ago that we'll be arriving in Medicine Bow in about an hour, so we'll finally be done riding trains." She studied Rebecca for a moment and then suggested. "You know, my dear, you might want to reconsider your dress. While it's most becoming, and I do so admire the beautiful lacework on the collar and cuffs, it seems a bit…well, a bit too civilized for a stagecoach ride."

The young woman looked down at her dress and then at the sensible blue wool shirtwaist with buttons up the front that Kate was wearing. Rebecca touched a napkin to her lips and smiled at her table companions. "Well, you are absolutely right. I don't know what I was thinking." Then she laughed ruefully and declared, "I guess after two years of getting used to city transportation, I'd put out of my mind how rough-and-tumble stagecoaches are. Therefore, I had better get back to my berth to change my dress, then gather my belongings and get ready to disembark."

"Disembark?" Tad asked.

Rebecca smiled. "It means get off the train."

The boy made a face and then admonished, "Why didn't you say that? Why did you use such a fancy word?"

"Tad!" his mother scolded.

"No, Kate, he's quite right," Rebecca said. "I shouldn't be so…" She started to say "pretentious" but then realized that the word itself was pretentious. So she smiled and said instead, "fancy. I'll see you before we get off."

"That can't come fast enough for me!" Tad exclaimed.

Standing, Rebecca McBride merely smiled thinly and then headed back to her berth. *As far as I'm concerned*, she thought to herself, *this train could take all the time in the world to get to Wyoming, and it wouldn't bother me in the least.*

TWO

I n the Buffalo Horn Saloon in Medicine Bow, Wyoming, the gambler took his beer over to a table and then sat down. A thin layer of tobacco smoke hanging just beneath the ceiling drifted and curled through the room, then collected in a small cloud above the man's table. Noticing it, he wondered if it were some portent of doom: then he shook his head and laughed inwardly. *You're not getting superstitious in your old age, are you, Trey?* he asked himself.

In his early forties, Trey Wentworth was handsome in a rather tired and jaded way. But unlike most of the other men in the saloon, the gambler was clean—in fact, almost fastidiously so—and his dark hair and equally dark eyes were mirrored by the fashionable, even elegant black clothes he always wore. There was also an air about him, a way he had of being detached from everything and everyone...even himself.

He picked up a deck of cards with hands that clearly had never done a hard day's labor, spread the cards out, and adroitly turned the entire deck over by passing a card back across the top. After that he let the pasteboards waterfall from hand to hand, his long fingers working so adeptly that it almost appeared as if magic were at work. Then he shuffled them and began dealing an imaginary poker game, for there was no one else at the table to receive the cards.

He had been in Medicine Bow for two weeks now, and he had been so successful at the poker tables that he could no longer find anyone to play with him. With a sigh, he turned over all the hands, noting the fall of certain cards, then picked them up, reshuffled, and dealt again.

A train whistle sounded outside, breaking the silence of the room, and the bartender pulled out his pocket watch and looked at it rather pointedly, almost as if he were responsible for the arrivals and departures of the Union Pacific trains. At the same time, a couple of men at the bar nodded at each other, passing a silent signal between them. Suddenly Trey Wentworth heard the double click of a revolver being cocked, and he felt the cold metal of a gun barrel pressed against the back of his head.

"Mr. Gamblin' Man," a deep voice hissed from behind him. "You're just too damned good with them there cards for the likes of Medicine Bow."

Trey tensed and laid the cards down. He kept his hands facedown and in full view on the table in what he hoped was a gesture that clearly indicated that he would not try anything. Clearing his throat, he asked, "Is skill against the law in this town?"

"Your kind of skill is," the unseen man behind him

replied. "Now, we ain't exactly callin' you a cheater, you understand, 'cause if that's what you've been doin', there ain't none of us been able to catch you at it. Rest assured that if we had, we'd be stringin' you up about now, instead of doin' what we're doin'."

"I see," Trey said, able to breathe a bit easier. If they were not going to lynch him, then it seemed less likely that this man would pull the trigger and kill him by shooting him. Calmly, he began picking his cards up from the table. "I take it, then, that I am being run out of town?"

"That you are, mister," the man replied. "I reckon you just heard the train whistle?"

"I did."

"That train'll be standin' at the depot for forty-five minutes; then it heads on west. There'll be a stage leavin' the depot 'bout the same time, headin' north. We don't much care which form of transport it is you choose, but you're gonna be on one of 'em."

Trey grinned laconically and straightened his string tie. "Well, since I've about exhausted my welcome along the Union Pacific route, I'm going to have to start looking for virgin territory. Therefore, I guess I'll take the stagecoach north. May I at least go over to the hotel and get my bag?"

"No need for that, Gamblin' Man. We got it for you." So saying, the man dropped a leather valise beside Trey's chair.

"May I turn around, please? I would like to see the composition of this farewell committee."

"Sure, go ahead, turn around," the man agreed. "Ain't none of us got any reason to hide from the likes of you." He laughed, adding, "Aside from which, ain't no way you'd be able to walk out of the saloon without turnin' around—and you sure as hell are gonna be walkin' outta here."

When Trey turned, he saw that there were at least six men with the spokesman. He recognized every one of them—and had in fact played cards with each of them.

"Ah, Lewis," he said to the man holding the gun. "Is it because you couldn't fill an inside straight that you decided to take your frustrations out in this way? And you, Hugh"—he shook his head slowly, berating the man—"breaking a pair of jacks to go for a flush when the pair alone would have won the hand. Oh, and we mustn't forget Ralph, a man who thinks bluster and bluff will compensate for an inadequate hand."

"That's enough of all that," a well-dressed man said. Trey recognized him as Ed McCutchen, a businessman who had played often—and lost often. "You're trying to get us to fight among ourselves," McCutchen snapped, "but your tricks won't work. We are men of resolve, and we intend to see that you leave town."

Trey dropped his cards in his jacket pocket and then leaned down to pick up his bag.

"Well, then, you gentlemen of...resolve...I bid you good day," he said, nodding graciously at his sendoff committee. Standing, he strode quickly across the room, pushed through the batwing doors, and stepped out into the afternoon sun. He stood there for a moment, blinking at the unaccustomed brightness, and then headed for the depot a block away. This was a routine procedure with him by now. Medicine Bow was not the first town he had ever been asked to leave.

———

As the train rattled to a stop at the Medicine Bow station, Kate Langston and Rebecca McBride gazed out the window, each lost in her own thoughts. Both women looked out at the same scene: a station platform stacked with crates and boxes and, beyond that, a dirt street, and a scattering of perhaps thirty low, unpainted, clapboard buildings. But though both saw the same things, they perceived them differently.

To Rebecca, this was the exact opposite of the life she had been living and enjoying in Boston, and she resented the injustices that had forced her to return to what she thought of as a godforsaken place. Kate, on the other hand, welcomed the sun-bleached buildings, the dust-covered men and women, and the heat waves radiating off the endless, empty plains. They were old and familiar things to her, and they had tightened their hold so securely around her heart that, seeing them now, she knew she would never leave them again.

The depot was a flurry of activity and noise. On the platform, men yelled at each other as a steel-wheeled cart was rolled up to the baggage car to load and unload suitcases, crates, and mailbags. Here the train also took on water, precipitating a great deal of banging and clanging of tank covers and waterspouts as the engine's reservoir was filled. The fireman kept the fire stoked and the steam going, and the rhythmic opening and closing of the valves as the pressure repeatedly built up and then vented away sounded remarkably like the laborious breathing of some great beast of burden.

In addition to those people manning the depot, and the train, and the passengers arriving and departing— plus those meeting them or sending them off—dozens of townspeople, to whom the arrival of the train was a major event, crowded the depot. This particular train also corresponded with the arrival and departure of the stagecoach heading north, lending an even more festive air to the occasion.

A few of the more urbane transcontinental passengers, those going on through to San Francisco, got off the train to stretch their legs and have a look around. Standing on the platform, they gawked at the local men lounging against the wall of the depot, their hips adorned with cartridge belts and pistols. The visitors stared unabashedly at the locals, for these were real "cowboys" of the type they had only read about, and they watched closely, waiting for the sudden explosion of temper that might lead to one of the famous gunfights that they presumed occurred regularly in towns like this one.

A few moments later, when a drayman popped his whip with the explosiveness of a pistol shot, several of the easterners jumped. Their eyes wide in fright and fascination, they drew closer together, the better to stay out of the path of any flying projectiles from the gunfight they were sure had broken out.

Laughing softly, Kate remarked to Rebecca, "I

suppose none of these city slickers have ever heard a bullwhip before."

"I suppose not," Rebecca agreed, also laughing. Though she had lived with easterners for the past two years and had even come to regard herself as one of them, she could not help but smirk at their tenderfoot reaction, and she felt a sense of superiority over them.

"Mama, I don't feel very good," Tad suddenly moaned, holding his stomach.

"Oh, dear! I just don't know what's wrong with you," Kate replied, kneeling, and putting a hand on her son's cheek. "Why don't you go over there and lie down on that bench, while I get our stage tickets?"

"I'll stay with him until you get the tickets; then I'll get mine," Rebecca volunteered.

"Thank you. That's very sweet of you," Kate sighed, standing and drawing her cream-colored shawl tighter around her shoulders, warding off the morning chill.

The ticket office for the stage line was inside the railroad depot. Kate arrived at the door leading into the building at the same time as a man dressed in black. The man smiled graciously, stepped back, and opened the door for her.

"After you, madam," he said.

"Thank you."

Kate bought tickets for herself and Tad to Buffalo, then, head down, she stepped aside to put them in her reticule. As she pulled the drawstring tight, about to head out of the depot, she was surprised to hear the man who had been behind her buy a ticket to the same destination. Turning, she saw that it was the same man who had held open the door.

She smiled at him, asking, "Do you live in Buffalo?" Then she laughed nervously. "I'm sorry. I know it was rude of me to inquire, but I used to live in Buffalo, and now I'm going back home. I was just wondering if we were neighbors."

"I couldn't think of anyone I would rather be neighbors with," the man said, touching the brim of his flat-crowned black hat as he smiled at her. "But the truth is, I'll be visiting your fair town for the first time."

"Oh," Kate murmured. She found the man intriguingly handsome, and the more she talked with him, the more certain she was that she was making a fool of herself. "Well, I, uh, I'm sure you will enjoy it," she remarked diffidently. "If you'll excuse me now, I must see to my son. You see, I'm a widow and—" Kate stopped midsentence and felt her face burning in embarrassment. She wished a pit would open up and swallow her whole. *Why* had she told him she was a widow? How obvious could a person be?

But the man smiled with seemingly genuine pleasure and said, "My name is Trey Wentworth. May I inquire as to your name?"

"Kate. That is, Kate Langston."

"Mrs. Langston, as we'll be traveling companions, and you are without a husband, I do hope you will call on me if you should need any assistance."

"Uh, yes, thank you," Kate mumbled, unable to meet his gaze. "But I'm sure I will have no difficulty."

"Nevertheless, madam, I shall remain at your service."

The redhead nodded and then scurried to the door.

Waiting for Kate to return, Rebecca McBride saw a tall, slim young man come out of the depot building. For a moment she thought she recognized him, and she half stood and raised her hand to call out to him. Then the young man turned his head, enabling Rebecca to see him more clearly, and she realized he was not who she thought he was. But then, of course, how could he have been? The person she thought he might be was dead.

It had taken her a long time to get over the guilt of his death. Not that she was responsible for it—she had had nothing to do with it—but she had been living a lie, never once finding the courage to end it.

They were to have been wed. He thought she loved him—and at one time, she thought so as well. Then she met another, and though propriety and honor would never let her declare that love, nor accept it had it been declared to her, she found that the face of the man in her most troublesome dreams belonged to *this* man, and not to the one she was pledged to marry.

The dilemma was solved for Rebecca in the cruelest and most tragic way when her betrothed had died, believing that Rebecca's love for him was as strong as his for her. That deceit troubled Rebecca far more than she could ever admit to anyone.

Not wanting to think about it, she glanced away from the handsome young cowboy and began talking with Tad Langston about the impending stagecoach ride.

———

Inside one of the houses on the other side of town, in the small residential section of Medicine Bow, Myron Haskell stood at the side of his bed, hurriedly packing his suitcase under the watchful eye of his wife, Nellie. Taking a shirt from a drawer, Haskell unfolded it and then refolded it, making absolutely certain that every crease was in the right place and no new wrinkles were being formed.

A short, thin man in his late thirties, Haskell had blue eyes, brown hair, and a small, closely cropped mustache. He was extremely fastidious looking, a trait even more evidenced by the great care he was taking with his packing.

Suddenly the bedsprings groaned in protest as his wife shifted.

"Myron?" she called.

"Yes, what is it? Can't you see I'm busy?"

"Myron, look at me."

Glancing at her, he found her looking at him with hurt eyes, and after a moment, she opened her mouth to speak.

Hesitantly, she said, "This pains me, but I have to ask it, Myron. Would you love me if my father wasn't the president of the bank and you weren't his chief clerk?"

"Nellie, what kind of a question is that?" Haskell demanded, sidestepping an answer. "Why, you degrade yourself—and me—by asking such things."

"I'm sorry, I can't help it," she replied. Her eyes misted over with tears. "Myron, I realize I am not a very pretty woman. But I could be a good wife to you if you would only let me."

"You are fine, Nellie. I have no complaints," he responded, his voice flat and cool. Finally putting his last pair of trousers into the suitcase, he closed it and buckled it shut.

"How long will you be in Buffalo?" Nellie asked with a sigh.

"I don't know," Haskell answered as he put his brown pin-striped jacket on and then tugged at the cuffs of his shirt. "Maybe as long as a month...or perhaps even longer. Your father has charged me with a very serious responsibility. As you know, this past winter was an extremely hard one in northern Wyoming, and many of the cattlemen were badly hurt. I will be handling a series of emergency loans, which is why I will be carrying a secret shipment of money with me—one of the largest ever transferred by the Medicine Bow Bank."

"Yes, I understand," Nellie murmured. Suddenly, she smiled and sat up on the bed. "Myron?"

"Yes, what is it?"

"What if I would come to Buffalo with you?" Nellie asked.

Haskell's face blanched. "Come with me? Are you crazy?"

"No, I'm not crazy," Nellie replied, unable to keep the hurt from her voice. "What is to keep me here? If you're going to be up there for an entire month, we could find a place to live, a small house perhaps, and you wouldn't have to stay in a hotel."

"No, it's out of the question."

"But won't you just—"

"I said it's out of the question," the little bank clerk repeated, holding his hand up to stop her from arguing any further.

"I just thought it would be nice," Nellie suggested.

Haskell forced himself to smile at her. "Yes, but think how much nicer it will be when I come home after being gone for so long," he said. "I have to have something to look forward to that will bring me back. Otherwise, I might decide I want to stay up there."

Nellie's eyes opened wide in surprise. Then she smiled when he laughed, intimating he was merely joking.

Brushing away her tears, she asked in a small voice, "Really, Myron? Will you really be looking forward to coming back home to me?"

"Yes, of course I will be. Now, I must be going. The stagecoach will be leaving soon."

"You'll kiss me goodbye?"

Walking up to the head of the bed, Haskell leaned over to give his wife a light peck on the cheek. He then hurried down the stairs and took his overcoat from the peg on the mirrored coat stand at the bottom of the stairs. He put on the coat, checked his appearance in the mirror and then left the house, walking briskly toward the depot, where the money would be delivered to him from the bank.

Across town, in Sheriff Archie Crawford's office, Seth Reardon picked up the old blue coffeepot from the stove and poured himself a cup of coffee. Like the man he was visiting, Seth also wore a sheriff's badge. He was the sheriff of Johnson County, far to the north, working out of the small town of Buffalo. He had brought three prisoners to Medicine Bow several days earlier, and they were now languishing in the back of the Carbon County-Medicine Bow jail.

Having been a lawman for more than half of his almost fifty-eight years, the tall, solidly built Reardon fit into his profession like a pair of old boots. He had an easy way about him and was usually as unruffled as his slicked-down gray hair, although his clear blue eyes could bore right through a man—especially those on the wrong side of the law.

"Well, Archie, I don't suppose you'll be needing anything else from me," Seth commented and then sipped the strong brew. "I believe I brought all the papers and such regarding those three miscreants, but if you find anything else is needed, let me know, and I'll send it to you."

"Well, it looked to me like you had everything in order, Seth," Archie Crawford replied. "But you know these judges. Sometimes they get peculiar ideas and start wanting things nobody's ever heard of before."

"You're telling me," Seth agreed in a dry voice. He took another sip of his coffee and then grimaced. "What did you brew this with? Axle grease?"

Archie laughed. "I like my coffee strong," he explained. "It helps keep me awake during long nights."

"If you'd hire yourself another deputy, you wouldn't have to work such long hours."

"Yeah, well, you tell that to the Carbon County

Board of Commissioners. I'm lucky to have what I got." He grinned, adding, "Fact is, if you want to know the truth, I'm glad your horse went lame and you're having to ride back to Buffalo on the stage."

Seth cocked his head and peered at his fellow lawman through narrowed eyes. "You want to tell me why my misfortune is making you so happy?" he asked.

"Because your misfortune is my good fortune—and it could be yours, too, if we play it right."

"All right, I'm listening."

"Nobody knows it yet, but there's going to be a very large shipment of money—one hundred thousand dollars, so I'm told—being sent up to Buffalo on the stage."

Seth let out a low whistle. "That's a fortune!" he exclaimed.

"Yes, it is. And the bank has offered a bonus to any deputy I can get who will ride up with the shipment. Now, the thing is, a deputy would have to go up there and come back...but you're going up anyway. If you was to agree to act as my deputy, I could pay you three-quarters of this bonus and pocket the rest for myself—and I wouldn't have to spare one of my men. I mean, you're going to be on the stage anyway, so what do you say?"

Seth Reardon took another sip of coffee and studied his fellow lawman over the rim of his cup. Archie was correct: He *was* going to be on that stage whether he accepted the deal or not, so if he could pick up a little extra for it, why not? And since he was going anyway, he could afford to take less than a special deputy, thus leaving some left over for the sheriff—and leaving the sheriff with all his deputies.

"All right," he finally said. He laughed and stuck out his hand. "It seems too good an offer to refuse. You've got yourself a deal."

"Good, good. I hoped you would do this. I figure we both stand to gain a little on this, don't you?" Archie Crawford paused and then remarked matter-of-factly, "Oh, by the way, I think there are a couple of things I should tell you."

"All right, what are they?"

"Well, to begin with, I just got word this morning that Brody Pike and his bunch robbed a bank over in Theresa a few days ago, killing a bank teller and one of the good citizens of the town in the process. That means they are very definitely on the prowl up there—and one hundred thousand dollars might well bring 'em out."

"The money shipment is supposed to be secret, is it not?" Seth asked, perplexed.

"Yes."

"Then if we're lucky, Pike and his bunch won't even know about it."

"True. Oh, but there's one more thing," Archie said. "It's Clay Donovan?"

"Clay Donovan? What about him?"

"He escaped from prison a few days ago."

"Did he kill anyone?"

"No." Archie then laughed, explaining, "He put on Earl Finley's duster and hat, stole his horse, and rode out of jail as slick as a fare-thee-well. I tell you one thing, you gotta give that boy credit for gumption, for all that he's a bank robber."

"He's not a bank robber," Seth snapped.

Archie laughed again. "Well, there's a judge and jury that'd disagree with you. They said he is, and that's why he was put in jail."

"I never for one minute believed he was guilty," Seth remarked, his weathered face sobering. He stared into the coffee cup gloomily and then took a last sip.

Sheriff Crawford stroked his chin and studied Seth for a long moment and then remarked, "That's right, come to think of it. You were one of those who testified for him, weren't you?"

"Yes."

"But all of them eyewitnesses saw him."

"No, they didn't. They saw a bunch of men riding out of town at full gallop with their guns blazing. Hell, Archie, you've taken a bunch of town folk on posses, and you've seen 'em in gunfights. Half of 'em close their eyes when they shoot. You tell me how anyone can make a positive identification of someone who's a hundred yards away, while at the same time trying to dodge bullets."

"Well, what about the marshal?" the lawman asked.

"He's not really a marshal; he's just a town constable. And if you'll pardon my language, he's about as worthless as tits on a chicken."

"You have a way to explain the evidence?"

"It was planted there," Seth said flatly.

"By the marshal?"

"Hell, no. He's too ignorant to come up with

anything like that. Besides, just because he's dumb, that doesn't make him dishonest. No, I'd bet my boots that Brody Pike did it."

"Maybe you're right, Seth," Archie mused after a moment. "But I don't reckon it makes any difference at this point. Whether Clay robbed that bank or not, he's now guilty of breaking out of jail."

"Yeah, I know," Seth said with a sigh. "And if I see him, I'll bring him in."

———

Brody Pike was sitting on a boulder near Clay Donovan's dead mount, idly tossing a rock from hand to hand, when the others came back from their search. Standing, the outlaw leader let the rock fall from his fingers and asked, "Find anything?"

"Nary a trace," Slim Hawkins answered. "I don't know who that was last night, but he got away cleaner'n a whistle."

"Yeah, well, he might've got away, but he's gonna have a hard time makin' it outta here on foot," Pike snorted. "Besides which, he ain't even got his canteen with him." Gesturing with his thumb at the gear by his feet, he remarked, "Lookee here. He left it hangin' from his pommel." Lifting the canteen, he added, "I checked over all the other gear and took what I wanted. You boys can have the rest if you want it." Stowing the gear in his saddlebags, he then remounted.

"Wonder who the guy was," Jim Porter said, shoving his hat back on his head.

"Probably just some fella wantin' to collect reward money," Pike replied. He laughed, adding, "I reckon he's learned by now that wantin' and collectin' is two different things."

"Pike, you reckon he heard us talkin' about the one hundred thousand dollars?" Slim Hawkins asked.

"I don't know," Pike admitted. "But even if he did, it don't make no never mind."

"He could maybe warn the folks with the money that we'll be comin' after it," Slim suggested.

Pike laughed, although the laughter never reached his cold dark eyes. "You think that anybody's gonna try and move that much money through here without already knowin' we'd come after it?" He shook his head. "Anyway, the bank's plannin' on keepin' it secret, so whoever that was nosin' around in the dark last night wouldn't have no idea who to give the warnin' to." Reining his horse around, he commanded, "Come on, boys, let's get a move on. We got some ridin' to do to be in position to pull this job."

"Are we just gonna give up on that fella that was sneakin' around last night?" Jasper Maddox wanted to know as they headed out.

"Yes. The man will either starve to death, freeze to death, or die from no water out here. It don't matter which way; he won't be botherin' us no more. You got my word on that."

———

Clay shielded his eyes and watched the bird. It was the fourth one he had seen alight at a particular spot. If all the birds had been the same kind, he would have presumed that there was a nest there, three-quarters of the way up the side of the rocky cliff. But they had all been different species, and that could only mean one thing: The birds were going to water!

Putting his hands on his hips, Clay studied the sheer rock wall. The place that was drawing the birds was at least two hundred feet above the ground, but though it would be a hard climb, he believed he could do it.

It would be easy, he thought, if he just had a rope. Then he mocked himself, saying aloud, "Yeah, and if wishes were wings, frogs wouldn't bump their backsides when they jump." He took a deep breath and then let out a long sigh and started up the side of the cliff.

It was very hard going. When Clay had been at it for roughly a half hour, he looked up toward his destination and groaned. It did not seem that he had gained so much as an inch. However, when he looked back toward the ground, he realized that he was making some progress, for by now he was dangerously high.

Clinging to the side of the mountain, he moved only when he had a secure handhold or foothold—tiny though it might be. Sweat poured into his eyes, and the thirst that had driven him to this state of desperation had been greatly intensified by his efforts. If he was wrong—if the birds were not leading him to water —he had made his situation even worse. He was so desperate for water now that he could feel his tongue swelling in his mouth.

Abruptly, Clay came to what appeared to be an impasse. He had progressed four-fifths of the way around a very large outcropping, but now he was stopped because he was unable to find another foothold. Clinging with hands that were fast becoming painfully swollen, he tried to figure out what to do next.

After five minutes, the young rancher reluctantly decided to start back down to see if he could find another way around the obstacle. Reaching for the handhold he had surrendered a few minutes earlier, he then put his foot down on the small slate outcropping that had supported his weight on the way up. This time, however, the slate failed, and with a sickening sensation in his stomach, Clay felt himself falling. He threw himself against the side, and the jagged rocks scraped and tore at his flesh as he slid downward.

He flailed against the wall with his hands, and after a drop of some fifteen feet, his bloodied hands found the trunk of a juniper tree growing out of the cliff. Grabbing the tree, which, thankfully, supported his weight, he hung suspended in midair. His heart was pounding furiously as he looked down between his feet at the rocky ground some one hundred and fifty feet below. The piece of the slate outcropping that had broken under his weight was still in free fall. Moments later he saw a puff of dust as it smashed against the ground, and then he heard the sound as it broke apart upon impact.

Suddenly his body shifted downward, and he felt the tree giving way. Cold sweat broke out on his brow and his palms. Frantic, Clay examined the cliff face and saw that about four feet away to his right was a narrow shelf. If he could gain that shelf, he would be all right. He took a deep breath and then swung his feet to the right and up—and missed. He felt his body fall another inch as the juniper's roots pulled out a bit more. *Dear God*, he prayed, *don't let me die like this! Not without clearing Vince's and my names!*

Straining with all his might, he swung his leg up again, but again he narrowly missed. He tried several more times, and each time the increased weight on the juniper tree pulled the roots farther out. Clay rested momentarily, listening to his pulse pounding in his ears. Then he tried again, and this time he caught the ledge with the heel of his boot. Breathing another silent prayer, he then slowly worked himself up, away from the juniper tree, until his knees were also on the ledge. Finally, he let go of the tree and pushed up slowly against the rock face until—and at last—he was safely on the ledge.

He sat there unmoving for a few minutes, gasping for air, and letting his heartbeat slow to normal. Then, when he had caught his wind and was ready to move on, he looked around and got a pleasant surprise. Rising up from the ledge was a "chimney," a narrow chute that shot straight up the side of the cliff. This natural shaft was studded with rocks in such a way as to almost form a ladder, and within a minute after starting up, Clay recovered the distance he had lost in the fall. The nauseating fear that had overtaken him earlier was now gone, and he climbed easily, finding footholds and handholds so conveniently located that it was almost as if they had been placed there for just such a purpose.

Finally Clay reached the spot where he had seen the birds alight, and he managed to leave the chimney and climb over to a large, flat rock. Just above the rock was a shallow cave, and there, trapped in a cool, shaded reservoir at the bottom of that cave, was a pool of water. With a happy shout, Clay dunked his head into the water and drank deeply.

The engineer blew two long whistles, the signal that he was releasing the brakes, and the train began rolling forward, steam gushing out of the drive cylinders on each side of the engine. Dozens of goodbyes were exchanged between those people who remained behind on the station platform and those who were on board, shouting through the open windows.

"Well, there it goes," Kate said, relief in her voice. She sighed. "It seemed like we were on that thing forever." Then she laughed and gestured across the platform, adding, "Though I guess by tomorrow morning, I'll wish we were back on it instead of that."

"That" was a Concord stagecoach. Tough and sturdy from its seasoned white ash spokes to its ox hide boot, it had no springs but was suspended on layers of leather strips, called thoroughbraces— making for a rough ride. The body of the coach was green, and the lettering on the doors was yellow, although the paint was tired and the colors faded, because the coach was at least ten years old and had seen a great deal of use during its lifetime. Still, it was well maintained, as evidenced by the neat and very skillful patchwork done to a few places on the coach body and the leather seats that had sustained some damage during its service. The coach belonged to the Wyoming Express Company, a stage line that connected outlying settlements throughout Wyoming with the railroads that passed through the territory.

Six horses were already in harness, and they stood quietly, awaiting the orders that would set them to their labors, drawing the coach north over the plains and mountains of Wyoming. A baggage cart laden with the passengers' luggage was pushed from the train over to the stage. Employees of the depot then began loading the bags onto the coach. They were able to get most of the pieces in the boot, though two large trunks, one belonging to Rebecca and one belonging to Kate, had to be lashed down on top.

The two women, one looking elated and the other glum, headed across the platform to the stagecoach. Audible sighs were heard from each as this last segment of their return home was about to begin.

THREE

As Rebecca McBride sat on the bench outside the depot, listening with half an ear to Tad Langston chatter on, she recalled that day in May two years before when she had left home. She had gone out to watch the sun come up one more time over her father's ranch, and even now she could remember how it looked as it climbed higher into the clear blue sky above the Rattlesnake Mountains. Looking down on the sweeping grandeur of the valley, its timbered foothills covered with blue pine and splashed with the rainbow colors of wild spring blooms, Rebecca had thought then that her father's ranch was the most beautiful place in the world. She had been sure that neither Boston nor anyplace else the East might have to offer could possibly match it.

Rising before dawn and dressing in denim trousers and a plaid shirt, Rebecca had ridden along the familiar ridgeline, picking her way up a trail that led to a secret precipice she had discovered as a little girl, and to which she often came when troubled or when she wanted to be alone. From the height of the rocky precipice, Rebecca could see the entire fifteen thousand acres of the finest rangeland in Wyoming Territory making up the Rocking M Ranch. This included the main house where she lived alone with her father, the bunkhouses where the forty ranch hands slept, and the barns, cookhouse, equipment shed, smokehouse, and assorted other buildings.

But the young brunette had gone up there to think, not to enjoy the beautiful view. Her betrothed was dead, and her father, thinking she could best recover from her grief in a new environment, had made arrangements to send her East to resume the schooling she had interrupted a few years earlier.

"It will be good for you to see some of the rest of the world," he had told her. "You should know that there are more places to be enjoyed than Buffalo, Banner, Ten Sleep, and Medicine Bow."

Rebecca had agreed to her father's recommendation. It was not so much that she was particularly anxious to see new places as it was that she felt she must leave this old place of pain and sorrow. For what her father did not know—and in fact what no one knew—was that while Rebecca did feel grief for her fiancé, she felt an even greater grief for the young man she really loved.

She had been able to attend the funeral of the one who had died, and there, she was comforted by friends. There, too, she had made her secret peace with the departed, begging his forgiveness for the guilt of her deception. But for the loss of her true love she had to grieve in secret, and she could not reveal to anyone that he was the one she really loved, not even to him. To have done so would have exposed her shame at the lie she had been living, and as circumstances had made it impossible to do anything about her true feelings, to have acknowledged them would only have intensified her pain.

As she sat on a fallen log, just on the verge of tears, she knew that she was closing the pages on that chapter of her life and preparing to go forward to what was yet to come.

In the valley below, a wispy pall of wood smoke had spread its diaphanous haze over the cookhouse, and Rebecca watched the cowboys, one at a time or in small groups, saunter to the cookhouse for their morning meal. She had seen her father walk out to the barn and begin hitching up the rig that was to take her into town that morning to catch the stagecoach to Medicine Bow, from where she would be able to connect with the train for the East.

She had known, even that morning, that she would be changed by her time in Boston, but she had not foreseen just how much. As she had looked down upon her father's ranch and the only home she had ever known, she had not imagined there would ever come a time when she would want to say goodbye to this place forever—yet that was exactly her thought as she sat there on the small wooden bench in the Medicine Bow, Wyoming, depot. For one odd moment, she almost wished she felt differently, but then she recalled the excitement, the vitality, of life in Boston, and she knew she was doing the right thing.

Rebecca had made up her mind. There was nothing for her there anymore, and she would not stay in Wyoming. If she could talk her father into going back to Boston with her, all the better. If she was unable to talk him into it, she was determined to go back anyway.

"Well, it looks like they've got the stagecoach all loaded and ready for us," Kate Langston announced, pulling Rebecca out of her reverie. "All we need now is a driver, and we'll be on our last leg home."

"Yes, I guess that's so," Rebecca agreed, suddenly feeling trapped in a netherworld between Boston and her father's ranch. She looked over at the coach and saw that the two young men who had been loading the luggage were now walking away. "It's our last leg home."

———

Across the street from the depot, driver Hank Bailey and his new shotgun messenger, Dingo, were eating dinner at the Prairie Skillet Restaurant. Hank was a regular there, and he told anyone who would listen that he considered the Prairie Skillet the best eating establishment in the entire territory of Wyoming.

In his early forties, with graying collar-length hair and a very long bushy mustache, Hank had been driving a stagecoach for nearly twenty years. Before that he had driven freight wagons, beginning his life-long profession at the age of fifteen. Nearly thirty years of sun and wind and heat and cold had weathered his face so that he looked even older than he was.

But looking older did not mean he looked frail or infirm, for Hank Bailey was a powerfully built man with wide shoulders, sinewy hands, and arms strong enough to rein a six-horse team with authority, yet skilled enough to impart subtle instructions to each horse through its own "ribbon" when that was needed. He was, without a doubt, most agreed, the best driver on the Wyoming Express Company's payroll.

Sitting across from his colleague, assessing him with his light-blue eyes, Dingo was a man whose age was more difficult to ascertain—he could have been anywhere from thirty-five to fifty—the determination not made easier by his sparse brown hair. A very short man, just a touch over five feet, Dingo was whipcord tough. Evidence of that toughness was the long scar that started under his right eye, came down over his cheek in an ugly, blue puff of skin and then ended in a fishhook, just under the corner of his mouth. Many people had asked Dingo how he had gotten the scar, but he always answered the query with an offhanded shrug. No one had ever had the poor sense to inquire further.

"Hank, would you be wantin' some more taters?" Evie Goodberry asked. She and her husband, Isaac, ran the Prairie Skillet Restaurant, and the big-boned woman in her early fifties asked the question with a large, easy smile.

"Don't mind if I do," Hank answered, sliding his plate over to her as she raked a new batch of fried potatoes from a black cast-iron skillet. "Nobody fries 'em as well as you, Evie."

The woman laughed. "Don't you be tellin' Lydia that," she quipped. "I wouldn't want your wife thinkin' you don't like her cookin'."

"Oh, Lydia knows I like her cookin' all right," Hank responded. "Fact is, the way I enjoy eatin', why, I reckon I would be kinda hard pressed to find somebody's cookin' I *don't* like."

"What about you, Mr. Dingo? You want anything else?" Evie asked the shotgunner.

"Wouldn't mind a few more beans," he answered, not meeting her gaze, and then he picked up a porkchop bone and started gnawing on it.

"You know, Dingo," Hank pointed out, "we're gonna have to take the run all the way to Buffalo without any relief drivers. We were supposed to change at the Powder River Station, but Cody's wife is over at Antelope Springs gettin' ready to foal, and he ain't gonna leave her."

"That's all right. It don't bother me none," Dingo said, shrugging. "If you wanna know the truth," he continued, "I'd just as soon go on to Buffalo than spend any time at Powder River, anyhow. There ain't a damn thing a fella can do at Powder River while he's waitin' for the next trip but sleep and swat flies."

"And smell the stink of oil," Hank added.

Nodding in agreement, the shotgunner remarked, "Which ain't good for nothin' but gettin' it all over you and makin' horses an' cows die from drinkin' the water."

Hank shook his head. "I can't help but feel sorry for all them poor beggars who homesteaded around there, then found that all their waterin' holes were polluted with that stuff. What good is that land to them?"

Evie came back from the kitchen carrying a pot of beans, and she spooned some onto Dingo's plate. "You boys be careful during this trip," she instructed. "You're gonna have a lot of money ridin' with you."

"A lot of money? What do you mean?" Hank asked, perplexed.

Pointing with her ladle through the front window, Evie asked, "You see that little feller there? The squinty-eyed, hollow-chested little man who's walking toward the stagecoach?"

Hank focused on the man and laughed out loud at the accuracy of Evie's description. He *was* a squinty-eyed, hollow-chested little man. "Yes, I see him."

"That's Myron Haskell," Evie explained. "He's the head clerk over at the bank, and he's married to Nellie Sampson—which means he's working for his father-in-law." She then proceeded to explain about the loans to the northern ranchers, concluding, "Haskell's taking the money up there personally—a hundred thousand dollars, from what I was told." She suddenly looked around, making sure no one was listening, and then concluded in a conspiratorial voice, "Only that's all supposed to be a secret."

"If it's a secret, how did you find out?" the driver asked.

Evie bent over the table and said quietly, "Well, Mr. Sampson and that Haskell fella have their lunch in here sometimes, and I overheard them talking. That's how come I know."

"Well, I'm glad to hear of it," Hank remarked.

"There was lots of fine folks hurt by the bad winter, and I know they'll be glad to see that some money's comin' in to tide 'em over."

"That may be, but if you ask me, the bank here sure picked out a weasel to handle all the dealings for them," Evie muttered. "'Course, as I said, Myron Haskell *is* Mr. Sampson's son-in-law, so I reckon he was the one had to be picked, being as he's family. But you tell them nice folks up there around Buffalo to be very careful whenever they're dealing with him. Don't go signing over the family ranch."

Hank laughed. "Evie, it sounds to me like you don't think too highly of Mr. Haskell."

"Let's just say that when he married Nellie Sampson, he came out a lot better on the deal than Nellie did—and I'm not just talking about the money."

Isaac Goodberry came out of the kitchen, wiping his hands on the apron that swathed his ample belly. Coming over to Hank Bailey's table, he laughed softly and put his hand affectionately on Evie's arm. "Is she bendin' your ear, Hank? Woman, come on now. Hank ain't got no time to be listenin' to all your palaver. He's got a stagecoach to drive."

"I was just tellin' him about—"

"I'm sure I know what you was just tellin' him about," Isaac interrupted. "Now go on. Them muffins you started bakin' need you back in the kitchen."

"All right, all right." Evie rejoined, sighing. She started to walk away from the table when she turned and smiled at Hank. "You be sure and tell Lydia I said hello, won't you?"

"I surely will," the driver promised.

"And you, Mr. Dingo, you come again next time you're in Medicine Bow."

"Yes, ma'am, I'll do that," Dingo also promised, still not looking up from his plate.

Isaac Goodberry watched his wife walk back to the kitchen and then shook his head, apologizing, "I'm sorry about all her gabbin', Hank. But you know how women love to chatter."

"Oh, I didn't mind at all," Hank insisted. Keeping his voice low, he continued. "Fact is, that was real good information she give me about Haskell, 'cause if somebody is plannin' on carryin' a lot of money with 'em on board my stagecoach, why, I'd sure like to know somethin' about it. If we're goin' to be waylaid, I damn well want to know what it is we're bein' waylaid for." He then stood and took a couple of coins from his pocket. "Here's for the supper for me an' my shotgun," he said. "And I'll be needin' a receipt if you don't mind."

"I don't mind at all. Was everything all right?"

"Real good." He looked at Dingo and smiled. "And from the looks of that spankin' clean plate, I don't reckon Dingo had any complaints either."

"It was real good," Dingo agreed, standing as well. "Say, Hank, I almost forgot what I was supposed to do before we head out. I'll meet you over at the stage in plenty of time."

"All right. Just don't make me have to wait none. The passengers get mighty upset if we ain't ready to go when we're supposed to."

"I'll be there," Dingo promised. Nodding to the restaurant owner, the shotgunner turned to leave. He pushed through the front door of the café, and despite his size—or maybe because of it—he had a swagger about him as he hurried out on his short, bandy legs.

"That's sure a little feller there," Isaac noted. "But judging from that scar decoratin' his face, I got me an idea that he ain't someone you'd be wantin' to get on your bad side."

"You've got that right," Hank said.

"I don't believe I've seen him before. Has he been with you long?"

"No, he just started workin' with the company," Hank explained. "Truth is, I don't really know too much about him—includin' his actual name. Dingo's all I know…and I don't know if that's his first name, his last name, or even if it's a real name. It might just be what he's chosen to be called."

"Where'd he come from?"

"Don't know that either," Hank admitted, rubbing his chin thoughtfully.

Isaac laughed. "You don't seem to know much about him at all."

"Well, I do know he's been around a bit. He's tended bar, worked as a hostler, deputied some, and been a cowboy. Dingo don't talk much when we're rollin', but he don't miss a thing on the trail. And when you get right down to it, what do you need to know about a shotgun guard anyway? All I really need from him is that he shows up on time, stays sober, and keeps his eyes open. And he does all that just fine."

"We know he's got a good appetite, too," Isaac observed, chuckling. He then tore a piece of paper from a writing tablet, jotted down a figure, and signed it. "Here's your receipt," he said, handing the paper over to Hank.

"Thanks," the driver said, sticking it in his pocket. "The home office is real particular about this. Time was when I could just tell 'em what I spent for my meals, and they wouldn't say nothin'. But some folks along the line was beginnin' to take advantage of it. And besides that, prices is gettin' so high nowadays. I mean, who'd have ever thought it'd cost a fella twenty-five cents just to eat a meal?"

Smiling at the restaurant owner, Hank put on his hat and promised, "I'll be seein' you on my next trip down. It don't matter what it costs, it's still the best food in the whole of Wyoming Territory."

"I'm glad you think so. And stay out of trouble," Isaac called as Hank left the café.

As the driver walked across the street, he saw that the luggage was already loaded—which meant he would not have to handle it. "Good," he murmured to himself. "I'm getting too old to haul them trunks up top."

The passengers who would be taking the trip were standing on the platform near the stagecoach, waiting for the driver and shotgun guard to show up. The small bank clerk, Myron Haskell, was holding a black satchel to his chest, and he paced back and forth nervously. Hank figured Haskell had to be carrying the money in the case from the way he was clutching it possessively. Laughing to himself, the driver thought that the banker was so small that anybody who wanted it could probably jerk the bag away from him, no matter how tightly he held onto it.

Haskell approached Hank Bailey as he neared the stagecoach. "It's about time you arrived," he remarked petulantly. "Come on, let's go. We can't wait around here all day."

Hank pulled the watch from his pocket and looked at it. "Take it easy, Mr. Haskell. We have eight minutes yet."

"You know my name?" Haskell said.

"You was pointed out to me."

"Then no doubt you also know that I am a person of no small importance in this town. And I'm not used to waiting."

"We ain't goin' nowhere till my shotgun messenger gets here."

"Well, where is he?"

"He went to do an errand."

The bank clerk was about to say something else when a woman's voice called out, "Hello, Hank."

Turning, Hank was surprised to see that one of his passengers was Kate Langston. He smiled broadly and walked over to her. "Kate! Well, now, if you ain't a sight for sore eyes!" he declared. "Do I assume that you're going to Buffalo?"

"I sure am. On your coach."

"Well, now, that's really fine news," Hank said, hooking his thumbs in his belt loops as he studied the beautiful redhead. His voice was filled with delight as he added, "Lydia's gonna be real happy to see you again. You always was just real special to her. How long are you goin' to be visitin' with us?"

"I'm not visiting," Kate explained. "I'm moving back home. I didn't like Philadelphia, so I'm going to reopen the hotel and live in Buffalo."

"You don't say! Why, look here, that's wonderful!"

Hank then smiled down at Tad and ruffled the boy's red hair. "And I'll tell you somebody else that's gonna be right happy to hear this," he told the boy. "Tad, would you believe that since you left last year, Jeff hasn't been able to find himself another best friend?"

"I can be his best friend again," Tad declared, smiling.

"Why, I know Jeff will be all for that."

Rebecca McBride then stepped forward and said, "Hello, Mr. Bailey."

"Ah, Rebecca, girl, you are even more beautiful now than you was when you left us!" Hank exclaimed. "City life sure seems to have agreed with you. Your pa told me you was gonna be on this train. He's really been lookin' forward to your comin' back."

"Yes, well, we'll see how he feels about it when I tell him what I have to say," Rebecca responded, sighing. "You see, the truth is that city life agrees with me a lot more than life out here. I'm going to stay only as long as it takes to convince my father to sell the ranch and move east."

"Well, now, why in heaven's name would you want to do a thing like that?" Hank asked, surprised by her suggestion.

"Because, unlike everyone in this godforsaken place, people back East live like human beings."

"Oh, I see," Hank said. He stroked his long

mustache as he studied her. "Well, I'm just real sorry you feel that way, Rebecca. And as far as you talkin' your pa into leavin' us out here, well, I'm afraid I can't wish you much success on that. All us folks around Buffalo regard your pa with a lot of affection, and I don't think there's anybody who'd care to see him just pack up and move away."

Suddenly Myron Haskell positioned himself in front of Hank Bailey and, ignoring Rebecca McBride, pointed across the street, asking, "Driver, is that your shotgun messenger coming out of the Western Union office there?"

"Yes, it is," Hank said.

"Then there's no reason for any further delay, is there?" Haskell fumed.

"No reason at all," Hank answered easily, a patronizing smirk on his face. Addressing the passengers, he suggested, "All right, folks, if you're all ready, climb on board, and we'll get started."

While the driver stood watching, the two women and the boy boarded first and then Myron Haskell began to climb inside. Dingo reached the stagecoach just as Seth Reardon passed Hank. The driver greeted his shotgunner, and then he nodded at the lawman, saying softly, "Sheriff, I'm glad you're riding with us. It turns out that one of our passengers is carrying a lot of money this trip, so it'll be good to have extra protection."

Seth stopped in his tracks and stared at Hank Bailey. "How did you know about the money?" the lawman asked, clearly taken aback. "It was supposed to be kept secret."

"Hell, Sheriff, it's our business to know," Dingo replied, answering for Hank.

Trey Wentworth, who was standing just in front of the sheriff, looked back over his shoulder and added, "Judging from the way the little gentleman is gripping that black bag, I'd say there's a vast sum inside." He pointed to Haskell's satchel.

The lawman gaped at Trey. "And *you* even know *who* it is! How in blazes has everyone found out about this? Is there a big sign on the side of the coach?" Seth asked sarcastically.

Trey laid his finger alongside his nose and smiled. "Let's just say it's a matter of professionalism," he replied. "I'm a gambler, you see, and money is my stock in trade. I can smell it."

The gambler and the lawman got into the coach. Trey, Haskell, and the sheriff settled down in the rear-facing seat, while Kate, Rebecca, and Tad sat in the forward-facing one. The boy was between the two women, lying with his head in his mother's lap and his feet in Rebecca's lap, and the expression on his face bespoke his discomfort.

However, when Trey Wentworth settled into his seat, the look on the boy's face changed to amazement. "Mister," he asked quietly, "can you really smell money?"

Trey laughed heartily. "Well, maybe I overstated my talent just a bit. I wouldn't actually want to be put to the test."

"You mean you *can't* smell money?" Tad asked, his disappointment evident.

Chuckling, the gambler admitted, "I'm afraid not."

Tad frowned. "Then why did you say you could?"

"Tad!" Kate Langston scolded, unable to keep the laugh out of her voice. Putting a finger to her son's lips, she told him, "Hush now. It's just an expression, that's all."

The child looked first at his mother and then at Trey. "Oh," he murmured.

"Folks," Hank Bailey announced as he held his hand on the door, ready to close it, "I hope you kept out somethin' warm to wear at night. It's mild enough in the daytime, this bein' May and all, but come dark, you're gonna think you're in the dead of winter. There's still ice in the cricks at night."

Murmurs of assurance rose from the passengers, and then Hank closed and latched the door and climbed up to the box. Dingo was already on top, sitting at his place on the seat with a rifle cradled across his lap. Settling in beside him, the driver released the brake and then took the whip from its holder and popped it over the team's heads. The coach immediately started forward, and within minutes they had rolled down the main street of Medicine Bow and reached the outskirts of town, traveling a little faster than what would be a man's brisk walk.

———

As the stagecoach rolled north, Trey Wentworth leaned his head back against the seat. He closed his eyes and listened as Rebecca McBride began telling Kate Langston a story about an adventure she had experienced while in Boston. Soon the gambler dozed off, and he found himself dreaming a dream he had had many times before. Coincidentally the dream concerned a young woman about the same age as Rebecca, and it took place in Boston. Trey was able to anticipate with great trepidation the terrible sequence of events as they unfolded, although he was forced each time to relive the images as if he were viewing them for the first time.

The dream would always start the same way. He was in a room near the Boston harbor, and he could hear a bell in a buoy clanging, its syncopated ringing sounding a repeated warning. The traffic outside was muted by the fog, and even the clip-clopping of horses' hooves on the cobblestones was barely audible. Inside the brightly lit room was a young woman who was clearly frightened, but Trey was telling her that she had absolutely nothing to fear.

"I make you a solemn promise that everything will be just fine, Christine," he reassured the beautiful brunette in his dream. "I give you my guarantee."

"And if it isn't all right?" the young woman always replied, a note of irony in her voice. "How will I be able to call in the guarantee?"

Suddenly the images shifted in time and space, and at this point in the dream, Trey would be shivering and sweating at the same time, finding himself looking down at a woman's bloody, lifeless body. His hands would be covered with the woman's blood as he held them up in front of him and cried out in agony, "No… no! My god, what have I done?"

"Mr. Wentworth? Mr. Wentworth, are you all

right?" a woman's voice called, wrenching Trey from his troubled sleep.

Opening his eyes, the gambler sat up with a start, realizing that he was a passenger in a stagecoach two thousand miles from Boston. His cold, shivering hands were raised in front of him, and the other passengers were all staring at him. The women had expressions of concern and compassion on their faces, while the men and the boy looked surprised and dismayed.

"Mr. Wentworth?" Kate Langston asked. "Are you all right?"

Recognizing hers as the voice that had spoken to him moments before, Trey forced himself to smile. "I apologize to you, Mrs. Langston—indeed, to all of you. I'm fine. It was merely a bad dream."

"You're sure you are all right?" she pressed.

"Yes, quite," Trey said. "I thank you for your concern, but really I'm all right."

Leaning back against the seat, he stared out the window, trying as hard as he could to blot out the painful memory.

FOUR

There were no streetlamps in the little hamlet of Soda Lake, Wyoming. It was much too small for such civilized amenities. The lights the stagecoach passengers had seen from a distance as they switch backed down the mountain road had come from the handful of buildings: a hotel and restaurant, a general store, a saloon, and a livery stable that also served as the stage station. In addition to the five commercial buildings, there were perhaps a dozen houses.

The coach clattered into town, the light from its twin kerosene sidelights illuminating the dusty street. Finally it drew to a stop in front of the livery stable and the lantern hanging on the sign to illuminate it also dimly lit the inside of the coach.

"Tad, wake up, honey, we're going to spend the night here," Kate Langston said.

Tad sat up and rubbed his eyes. "Where are we, Mama?" he asked, his voice slurred with sleep.

"We're in Soda Creek," Kate answered. Pointing through the window, she explained, "We're going to go across the street and get a room in that hotel over there."

"Kate, I can go on ahead and get our rooms," Rebecca offered.

"Thank you. I'd appreciate it," Kate responded. Then she looked down at her son, asking, "Are you hungry, Tad? What would you like for supper?"

"I don't feel like eating," Tad groaned. "My stomach is hurting real bad."

"Still? Oh dear. I hoped it would have quit by now."

Trey Wentworth stepped out of the coach first, helped Rebecca down and then reached for Tad. He swung the boy down, and Tad winced as he was put on the ground.

"I'm sorry, son," Trey told the boy kindly. "I surely didn't mean to hurt you."

"That's all right," the boy assured him. "I think it just hurts now because I'm tired from sleeping." Looking at his mother, he asked, "Mama, do I have to go to bed right away?"

"Tired from sleeping, huh?" Kate repeated with a laugh. "Well, I'm glad to hear that. You can't be feeling too poorly if you're wanting to stay up."

Hank Bailey and Dingo climbed down from the top of the coach and stretched while a couple of hostlers hurried out to unharness the team and lead them off for food and water. Myron Haskell then stepped out and immediately crossed the street. He was followed out of the coach by Seth Reardon, who stood with the others. The men watched Haskell walk quickly toward the hotel, hurrying along behind Tad and Kate.

"Look at how tight that little feller is holdin' that bag. Wouldn't you hate to try and grab it away from him?" Hank asked with a chuckle. "He'd just give you the fight of your life."

The others laughed with him.

"Well, I for one hope nobody tries to take it away from him," the lawman remarked. "I'm getting paid extra to watch over him, and I'd like nothing better than for the trip to be peaceable."

From the saloon across the way came a woman's high-pitched shriek, followed by the laughter of a dozen or more men. After that a piano began playing, and the notes spilled through the batwing doors into the street. One cowboy came out of the saloon and started up the boardwalk away from the coach, while two other cowboys seemed to materialize out of the darkness in front of the saloon, pushing their way through the doors to go inside. The Broken Spur Saloon was the most brightly lit building in town, and it seemed to draw the cowboys to its glow with the same magnetism with which the gleaming kerosene lanterns here and there were drawing fluttering moths.

"Hank, do you stay in the hotel when you spend the night in this town?" Seth asked.

"No," the driver answered. He stretched and yawned and then scratched his head, ruffling his hair. The company keeps a room for me and my shotgun guard in the back of the livery. Tell the truth, though, it ain't all that invitin', and sometimes I just slide the seats together in the coach and stay in there. It makes up into a fine bed if there ain't no more'n two or three tryin' to use it."

"You plannin' on doing that tonight?" the lawman queried.

"No, not if you're wantin' to save a little money by usin' it," Hank offered generously.

"Well, I appreciate that. Maybe I will just sleep in the coach."

"Sheriff, if you don't mind some company, I'll stay in the coach with you," Trey declared. He looked over toward the Broken Spur Saloon, adding, "I'd rather spend my money on drink than sleep anytime."

Seth laughed. "Can't say as I blame you. I could use a little snort myself. What say we mosey on over there and have one or two?"

———

Rebecca McBride had managed to get adjoining rooms for herself and the Langstons. Stopping first in the hotel dining room for supper, the three travelers then went upstairs to their rooms on the second floor.

With the door between their rooms standing ajar, Rebecca washed her face and hands at the basin on the table in her room, while in the next room Kate was sitting on the edge of the bed, looking after Tad. After barely touching his meal, the boy was complaining that his stomach was hurting more than ever.

"You know, Rebecca," Kate called, "I'm really beginning to be worried about him. It isn't at all like him to be sick like this, and if it had simply been train sickness or something he ate earlier, I should think it would be over by now."

Putting down the towel, Rebecca rebuttoned the several buttons she had opened on the neck of her red plaid wool dress and walked into the adjoining room. She leaned over the boy, feeling his face and then remarked softly to Kate, "I'd say he has a slight fever. Tell you what. I'll go downstairs and ask the hotel clerk if there's a doctor in town, and if there is, I'll send for him and then come right back."

"Oh, would you? I'd be very grateful," Kate said, her face pale with worry.

Rebecca hurried down the stairs and then across the lobby to the front desk. The middle-aged clerk was reading a newspaper by the lamp on his desk, and he lay the paper aside and began preening his thick mustache as the beautiful young woman approached.

"Well, now, little lady," the clerk said, "what is it I can do for you?"

"Is there a doctor in this town?"

"Well, there's Doc Harmon," the clerk said. "Some folks don't think too highly of him, but if you'd like, I could run him down for you."

"Thank you, but the doctor isn't for me," Rebecca explained. "I want him for my friend's little boy, who's having terrible stomach pains."

"The little boy, huh? Well, I reckon whatever ails the boy won't tax Doc's skills none. I'll go get hold of him and send him on up to the boy's room."

"Thank you," Rebecca replied. "The room number is—"

"We're not that full, miss," the clerk interjected,

smiling easily. "You're in two-oh-four, and the boy and his mama are in two-oh-two. Is that right?"

"Yes. How long do you think before the doctor will get here?"

"Very soon, I would think. He's probably just over at the saloon."

"Thank you very much for your kindness," Rebecca said, giving the clerk a sweet smile.

Rebecca started back up the stairs, and as she did so, Myron Haskell was coming down. Haskell put his hand up, stopping her progress. He then took a long, slow, appraising look at Rebecca, examining her from head to toe with such unabashed intensity that it made her uncomfortable.

"I was wondering if, uh, perhaps, we might have a drink together?" he asked.

His question surprised Rebecca. "A drink? I'm afraid not. Thank you for asking, but I don't imbibe."

"I see," Haskell mumbled. "Well," he went on, putting his hand on her forearm, "I want you to know that if there is anything I can do for you, you'll find me just a few rooms down from your own." His hand began moving up and down, caressing her arm.

"Thank you," Rebecca responded coolly, pulling away resolutely. "I'm sure I'll be able to handle everything just fine."

She turned, about to continue on up the stairs, but Haskell continued talking. "I listened with pleasure to your stories about Boston," the clerk said. "It must be a wonderful place."

"Yes, I liked it."

"I'm sure a young woman such as yourself could have a pleasant time in a city like Boston."

"Yes, I suppose so," Rebecca replied. She did not like the conversation, and she did not like the salacious gleam in the man's eyes.

"And if a young woman...say a very beautiful young woman such as yourself...were to play her cards right with a man with a very bright future...say, someone like me...then she might find the city even more enjoyable, don't you agree?"

He put his hand back on her arm and began caressing it again.

"A woman like me with a man like you?" Rebecca snapped. "That could never be, Mr. Haskell."

Haskell's face grew dark and the fingers of his gently caressing hand suddenly clamped down on her arm. "And what is wrong with a man like me?" he asked, his voice threatening. "Are you saying that I am not good enough for you?"

"No, Mr. Haskell. I am saying you are married," Rebecca replied easily, "and now would you please let go of my arm? You are hurting me."

Haskell seemed astonished by her behavior and released his grip instantly. "Yes, yes, of course. Please, forgive me," he muttered. He smiled. "You are right of course. I am married, and that's why I meant nothing...improper...by my question. I was just suggesting that the time may come when you may need a friend, and I am offering myself in that capacity."

"Thank you, Mr. Haskell. I shall keep that in mind," Rebecca told him coldly. "And now, if you will excuse me, I really must go see what I can do for Mrs.

Langston." Without giving him time to respond, she turned and hurried up the stairs.

A few minutes after Rebecca had returned to Kate's room, a knock sounded on the door and the young woman opened it. A short, fat, rather disreputable-looking man stood there, and Rebecca's face fell. She had been expecting the physician.

"You asked for a doctor?" the man asked.

"Yes," Rebecca replied, sighing. "Couldn't he come?"

"Madam," the man countered, pulling himself up indignantly, "I am he."

The doctor had obviously been drinking, and though he did not appear to be drunk, he smelled strongly of alcohol. Rebecca had to take a step back to catch her breath—and to avoid his.

"Where is the child?" he asked.

"He's here, Doctor," Kate called from farther back in the room. She was sitting on the edge of the bed, holding a damp facecloth to Tad's forehead. "There's something terribly wrong with him. I think it's far more than a simple stomachache."

"Are you a doctor, madam?" he asked, somewhat churlishly.

"What? No, of course not."

"Then kindly leave the diagnosis to me," Dr. Harmon sniffed, moving over to the bed.

Rebecca watched him warily. In addition to being short and fat, his skin was red and blotchy, and while in compliance to convention he was wearing business clothes—a long, dark coat, lighter pants, a vest, and a string tie—his clothes were extremely unkempt. In fact he had such an altogether unhealthy appearance that Rebecca thought her first impression of his being a messenger from the saloon who normally swept floors and emptied spittoons was unfair to floor sweepers and spittoon emptiers.

The physician set his bag down on the dresser, opened it and then took out a flat stick. Putting the stick on Tad's tongue he ordered brusquely, "Say ah."

"Ahhh," Tad responded.

As the doctor examined him, he pushed the tongue depressor so far down into the child's throat that Tad gagged and then began crying.

"Young man, it's hard to look you over if you're gonna be such a crybaby," the physician mocked.

"Doctor, please," Kate complained, "he's only eight years old, and he isn't feeling well. And frankly, you aren't being very gentle with that stick."

"Madam, if you don't like the way I'm doctorin', you can get another one," Harmon said. He put the stick back in his bag, and Rebecca wondered if that meant he planned to use it with another patient at some time in the future.

"Is there another doctor in this town?" Kate asked coolly.

"Not for fifty miles, ladies. Not for fifty miles," Harmon replied.

"Then we obviously can't get another one, can we?"

"Nope."

The doctor took a look at each of Tad's eyes and then measured his pulse. Rebecca glanced at Kate, and when their eyes met, they exchanged a look that said Harmon seemed to be acting professionally enough. Finally he completed his examination and stood up.

"Well, you can put your mind to rest, madam," he said to Kate. "Your boy doesn't have anything seriously wrong with him."

"Thank God," Kate responded, sighing.

"In fact, he's not suffering from any of the usual maladies that I can see. Perhaps the travel has made him somewhat irregular. That would give him a stomachache, sure as shootin'. I'll prepare a purgative for him. That'll clean him out well enough, and he shouldn't have any more problems. It'll cost you twenty-five cents. Do you want it?"

"Yes, of course, if that's what it takes to get him well," Kate replied.

Dr. Harmon looked across the room at the water pitcher. "Any water left in that jug over there, girl?" he asked Rebecca.

"Yes."

Harmon took a small, brown bottle from his bag and handed it to her. "Fill this bottle to about here," he said, indicating with his finger where he wanted it.

Rebecca did as directed and then handed the bottle back. The physician riffled through his medical bag and finally extracted an envelope. Opening it, he poured some white powder into the bottle, stoppered the bottle, gave it a good shake, and then handed it over to Kate.

"You go ahead and give him a good dose of it now, and then give him another just before he goes to sleep...and keep on giving it to him until he quits complainin'." Picking up his bag, the doctor said, "That'll be a dollar for my services."

Kate walked to the dresser for her reticule, reaching into it and extracting several coins. Handing them to the physician, she told him, "I really appreciate your coming over to the hotel to see him at this time of night, Doctor. And I am very glad that he isn't suffering from anything serious."

"Nothin' serious at all, madam," he assured her. Nodding to each of the women, he then left the room on slightly unsteady feet.

————

Over at the Broken Spur Saloon, the piano player was grinding out "Little Joe the Wrangler." One of the bar girls was leaning on the back of the piano, singing along off-key, but she was the only one who was paying attention to the music. At all the other tables and along the bar, the cowboys and assorted other patrons were engaged in so many loud, animated conversations that the piano and singer were barely audible.

Seth and Trey had a table near the door. The lawman took a swallow of his beer and studied the gambler over the rim of his glass. "You're the fellow the sheriff back in Medicine Bow told me they were running out of town, aren't you?"

"Yes," Trey acknowledged, nodding, a rueful expression on his face.

"And so now you're coming to my town?"

"That's my plan," the gambler admitted, grinning.

"Do you cheat at cards, Mr. Wentworth?" the lawman asked bluntly, his clear blue eyes staring intently at his companion.

"No," Trey replied. "Did your friend the sheriff accuse me of cheating?"

"Not exactly," Seth responded. He licked the beer foam from his upper lip and then continued, "Archie Crawford told me you were so good that you win damn near all the time, but he said that no one had ever been able to actually catch you cheating."

"That's because I don't."

"Then would you mind explaining how the hell you manage to win so often?"

"Sheriff, have you ever heard the expression, 'in the world of the blind, a one-eyed man is king'?"

"Yes, I have," Seth acknowledged, shifting his sturdy body in the chair to lean back.

"You are looking at living proof of that adage," Trey said. "Most men who play poker play it with their heart, with their temper—and with their pride." Touching the side of his head with his finger, he explained, "I play poker with my brain. Since I'm usually the only thinking man at the table, I'm generally the winner."

Seth laughed. "Well, I don't suppose a person could argue with that."

"An awful lot have," Trey rejoined with a snicker. "There's not a town along the Union Pacific that would welcome me back."

"I didn't figure Medicine Bow was the first town you'd ever been run out of," the lawman observed wryly. Leaning forward again, he took another swallow of his beer, finishing it, and then wiped the back of his hand across his mouth. "But I'll make you this promise. If you aren't cheating, you won't be run out of my town. Buffalo always has room for honest men."

"Well, I appreciate that, Sheriff," Trey replied. "I really do."

Suddenly there was a loud burst of laughter from the bar, and the travelers looked over toward the source. A short, fat man with a red face and big nose, who had come in a few minutes before, seemed to be the center of attention, and he was speaking in a very animated manner.

"Doc, you was in here tryin' to borrow the cost of another drink not mor'n a half hour ago," somebody shouted. "And now you got a whole dollar to spend. How'd you come by it?"

"I did a bit of doctorin' on that kid that come in on the stage tonight," Harmon answered. He put the dollar on the bar and watched attentively as the bartender filled a large glass with whiskey. Lifting the glass to his nose, he inhaled the aroma and then sighed with satisfaction just before he tossed the drink down.

"Ah," he breathed after a moment. "That was good, sir." He snickered, adding, "A damn sight tastier than that purgative I administered to the kid, I'd wager." Wordlessly, he held his glass out for more whiskey.

"What was wrong with the kid?" the bartender, a burly man in his thirties, asked.

The doctor laughed. "Aw, he was complaining of a

stomachache. But if you ask me, he's just a whiner who's been mollycoddled by his overprotective mother. There's nothin' wrong with him that a swift kick in the seat of the pants wouldn't cure."

Those around the doctor exploded in laughter as the doctor held out his glass yet again and then tossed down a third whiskey as quickly as he had the first two.

Overhearing the conversation, Trey Wentworth turned away in disgust and stared into his beer with an angry expression on his face. "Somebody needs to take that gentleman out to the barn and teach him a few manners," he grumbled.

Seth nodded. "I know what you mean," he replied. "When you share a long trip like this, the passengers sort of begin to belong to one another, like cowboys working on the same spread. If an outsider says something about one of us, it's like they're talking about all of us."

"That's true," Trey replied. "But it's much more than that. That man is a doctor—or at least he's supposed to be one. He should show more compassion for his patient. The cardinal rule of a doctor is 'first, do no harm.' For that man to administer a purgative without knowing what was wrong with Tad Langston is practically criminal behavior."

Suddenly the town doctor shouted, "Yep, I'd sure as hell like to be that little brat and have that good-looking woman caring for *me*! Matter of fact, I think there's nothin' wrong with the kid—it's the widow-woman who's ailin'! And what's ailin' her could be healed right quick!"

The physician's cronies roared with laughter.

Harmon continued, "Yeah, that there's one good-lookin' redhead. And I'm thinkin' that maybe I've got just the curative prescription for her!" He grinned salaciously and then shouted, "Me!"

Trey Wentworth slammed his glass on the table and started to rise, his dark eyes flashing. Seth Reardon grabbed his forearm, but the gambler shook off the restraining hand, saying, "I think this so-called doctor is the one who needs curing…of ill-mannered, boorish behavior."

"Are you sure you want to mess with him?" the lawman asked, keeping his voice low. "He's got a lot of friends—and they all may well back him up."

"That's a chance I'm willing to take," Trey said. His handsome face stiff with anger, he strode to the doctor's table and stood over him, glaring at him but saying nothing. Harmon finally looked up with watery eyes and asked in a besotted voice, "Something I can do for you, mister?"

"Yes," Trey replied coldly. "You can stop impugning Mrs. Langston."

"Mrs.…." The physician's face was puzzled. "Oh! You mean the luscious redhead!" He snickered. "Why? Is she a friend of yours? A *good* friend?"

Trey abruptly reached down and grabbed the doctor's shirtfront, lifting him out of his chair. "She is a mere acquaintance—and a very respectable one. I will thank you to say no more about her or about her son, who is quite ill, although a man of your lack of skill apparently cannot discern it. How you can call yourself a doctor is beyond me. You're a disgrace to the profession!" So saying, he released the man, flinging him down into his chair so hard that Harmon's teeth clacked together.

Several of the doctor's friends started to get out of their chairs but stopped immediately at the sound of a pistol being cocked. Trey glanced over his shoulder and saw Seth Reardon standing there, his Colt .45 trained on one of Harmon's friends.

"If any of you try anything, you'll have me to answer to," the lawman snarled. Pulling his jacket aside, he revealed his sheriff's badge, adding, "And as you can see, I've got the authority to use this weapon."

The men looked from the sheriff's face to his revolver to the badge on his shirt and then back up at his face. No one made a move.

Then suddenly Harmon stood up, so abruptly that his chair fell over, and he threw a punch at Trey Wentworth. But the drunken physician's aim was off, and all he got was air. Trey shook his head in disgust and started to walk away, but Harmon went after him. Grabbing the gambler's shoulder, he spun him around and then landed a solid right on Trey's jaw.

"You should have left well enough alone," the man in black growled. He then hauled back his fist and slammed the doctor hard on the chin. Harmon's feet went out from under him, and he landed on the floor with a thud. He started to rise, but then his head lolled for a moment before he lay prostrate, unconscious.

Flexing his fingers, making sure nothing was broken, Trey regarded his opponent sprawled on the sawdust-covered floor with his mouth hanging open. He was unsure whether the doctor had been felled by the punch or from drink—but then he did not much care. Satisfied with the outcome of the encounter, he nodded to Seth Reardon, who gave a warning glance at Harmon's friends and then accompanied the gambler out of the saloon.

———

Back in the hotel, Rebecca McBride and Kate Langston were discussing the journey. They were speaking softly, for Tad had finally fallen into a restless sleep on the bed behind them.

"I sure will be glad when we get home," Kate said. "Maybe a few days rest is all Tad needs. It seems as if we've been traveling forever."

"Doesn't it, though?" Rebecca said, shaking her head in disbelief.

Kate laughed. "And yet, it's only been a few days since Tad and I stepped onto the train in Philadelphia. When I think of all the people who made this long journey before the railroad was built—why, it makes me positively ashamed for feeling sorry for myself."

Rebecca mused, "My mother and father came west on a wagon train." She sniffed, adding, "They could hardly wait to get out here...and I can hardly wait to go back."

Kate smiled. "Oh, now, Rebecca, I wouldn't be so quick to decide that, if I were you. Perhaps you'll surprise yourself and come to feel that this is where you belong after all. Surely there are some things about it that you remember fondly."

"Oh, yes," Rebecca admitted. "Seeing that sunrise

this morning reminded me of all the sunrises and sunsets I used to enjoy on my father's ranch. And I remember the way the bighorn sheep would play on the mountainsides and the sounds of their hooves clattering against the rocks when they would break into a run." A faraway look came into her eyes, and she continued, "I always loved hearing the cattle late in the evening, when the cows would start calling out to their calves. And I confess that I miss being able to ride a horse...I don't mean ride a horse sidesaddle in a city park while wearing some stylish riding habit. I mean really ride like the wind, dressed in a man's denim trousers and shirt." The young woman's eyes sparkled brightly as she talked.

"See, what did I tell you?" Kate enthused, her auburn hair catching the light as she nodded vigorously. "You're going to find that you missed it out here more than you thought."

"No, I don't think so," Rebecca responded, playing distractedly with the tassel on her nightgown. She was quiet for a moment, and then she said softly, "I do miss all those things, that's true—in fact, I miss them terribly. But I'm afraid there's nothing here for me anymore."

Kate reached across the table and put her hand lightly on Rebecca's. "Dear, I know what you are feeling," she murmured. "I went through the same thing when my darling husband died. All I wanted to do was escape that place where we had lived together, escape it and the memories. But life does go on, after all, and I've learned now that there's more sweetness to the memories than there is pain. And who knows?

Perhaps there'll be another man in my life someday."
She smiled brightly. "If so, I wouldn't want that man
to be a Philadelphia dandy." Giggling, she concluded,
"I saw enough of those gentlemen this year to last a
lifetime."

Rebecca laughed. "How about a Wyoming
dandy?" she asked, her eyes twinkling mischievously.
"Someone like Mr. Wentworth, perhaps?"

"Rebecca!" Kate gasped.

"Now, don't tell me you haven't noticed him,"
Rebecca teased.

Blushing, Kate looked down at her hands for a
moment. Then she looked up and smiled broadly.
"Well, perhaps I did notice a little. But I think you're
wrong when you call him a dandy." A frown suddenly
creased her forehead, and she commented. "You know,
there's something about him that bothers me."

"Troubles you?" Rebecca asked.

"No, I wouldn't exactly say that it troubles me."
She sighed and then observed, "During all those years
my husband and I ran the hotel in Buffalo, I saw more
than my share of professional gamblers. I got to the
point where I could pick one out the moment he came
through the front door, no matter how he was dressed.
Now, I'm sure Mr. Wentworth is indeed a professional
gambler as he says, but I'm also sure that there is more
to that man than meets the eyes." She paused and then
added, "And I have to admit that he is quite a handsome man."

Rebecca countered, "Yes. Well, I suppose he is
handsome. Not as handsome as Mr. Haskell, of course,
but he is handsome."

"Not as handsome as Mr. Haskell?" Kate blurted. Then, because Rebecca had told Kate about the incident on the staircase, she realized that the young woman was teasing. She began laughing so hard that tears came. Finally she managed to get control of herself long enough to wipe the tears from her eyes and titter, "Oh, yes, Mr. Haskell is quite handsome—but, alas, we mustn't forget, as you reminded him, he is married."

"Oh, such is the pity," Rebecca managed to remark wryly before dissolving in laughter with Kate.

Finally, their laughter having subsided, the two women hugged each other affectionately and bid one another good night.

"We've got a long day ahead of us," Kate commented. She glanced over at her son. "I certainly hope that purgative will have helped Tad. The journey is uncomfortable enough, without feeling sick."

Patting her friend's shoulder just before she returned to her own room, Rebecca assured her, "He'll no doubt be just fine. You'll see."

FIVE

Using his hat, Clay Donovan fanned the sparks until the kindling caught. He was cold and he was hungry, but now he was finally about to relieve both conditions.

Within a couple of minutes the fire was burning, and he started tossing more twigs onto it until it was a fairly respectable blaze. That done, he tended to the rabbit he had managed to kill a shot time earlier, by the first light of dawn. The rabbit would be the first food he had eaten in two days, and he had been lucky to get it, for he had shot it with his very last bullet. Skinning it by using a sharp piece of shale, Clay then spitted it on a green twig and hung it over the flame.

A short while later, sitting with his back against the wall of the cave after devouring the last of his rabbit, Clay found himself thinking about his brother and about the future they had tried to build together. He and Vince had come West with their mother after the war, when both were very young children.

It had been a decision of necessity for his mother, for with her husband dead and two small boys to raise, Emma Donovan had to support her family, and she did so by teaching school. Though she had been a schoolteacher in Missouri before the war, the educational requirements to teach there had changed, and Emma was no longer qualified. Then she read a newspaper article noting that the western states and territories were so desperate for teachers that their educational requirements were not as strict. On the strength of that article, Emma moved her family to Colorado and taught for many years.

For as long as Clay could remember, he and Vince had wanted to own their own ranch, and when they were grown, they left home to pursue their ambition. There were several stops along the way in the early years. Clay had been a hired hand for other ranchers, he had driven a freight wagon and worked as a shotgun guard, and he had driven a stage. Finally, a couple of years earlier, he and Vince had managed to get a ranch started, and while it had been rough going in the beginning, they stayed with it.

It had always been their intention to bring their mother to Wyoming to live with them once they had the ranch established. That notion was brutally destroyed when, on the very dawn of their success, Vince had been killed and Clay sent to prison.

All the time he was in prison, Clay had received letters from his mother as regular as clockwork, for Emma never seemed to lose hope, and each letter would tell of some new plan she had for getting him released or some person she had contacted on his behalf. Then one day Clay got a letter from one of the lawyers she had been working with who informed him, with regret, that his mother had succumbed to a fever.

The sudden and unexpected death of his mother had hit Clay as hard as anything that had happened to him since he had been sent to prison. But ironically her death had led to his freedom, for Clay would never have tried to escape if his mother had still been alive.

Now Clay hoped his freedom would not end up being short-lived as a result of the decision he had reluctantly come to. Having at one point driven the stagecoach between Medicine Bow and Buffalo, he knew that it would be coming through this part of the country later that morning. He also knew that if he was going to survive, he had to meet that stage. The danger lay in the chance that he would be recognized, and if the people on the stage were aware that he was an escaped prisoner, he would have no choice but to give himself up. Even if he had had ammunition, he would not put up a fight. That would mean injuring or killing innocent people—and that was something Clay Donovan would never do.

———

It was barely light when the coach pulled out of Soda Lake, and all the passengers had reclaimed the same seats that they had occupied the day before. By now they had learned the skill of getting comfortable in a close and rough-riding coach, and they leaned their heads back, propped their feet against the seats opposite to minimize the jostling, and then quickly dropped off to sleep.

Trey Wentworth dreamed again, and again his sleep was troubled by disquieting visions from his past.

———

"Are you sure you want to go through with this?" a man in a surgical gown asked. "The malignancy has progressed much too far—and as you well know, such a procedure has never been tried before."

"Not in America, but it has been successfully demonstrated by Andral in Paris," Trey replied, looking down at the operating table. He then lowered the sheet that had been covering the face of the anesthetized patient—and it was the same beautiful young woman to whom he had given his guarantee that the operation would be successful.

The assisting surgeon shook his head. "Dr. Wentworth, I have the utmost respect for your surgical skills—but removing a malignant tumor is extremely difficult and removing it from the abdomen is nearly impossible. She may well die on the table."

Trey looked over at the assisting surgeon and replied levelly, "I gave her my word that she will come out of it successfully."

Shaking his head again, the assisting surgeon declared, "I pray that you won't live to regret a promise made in desperation."

Trey ignored the comment and picked up his scalpel to begin the delicate operation. All went well until he was about to close the abdomen, then suddenly the woman began to hemorrhage. Although the young doctor worked frantically to stop the bleeding, the woman's blood pressure dropped precipitously, and despite Trey's best efforts, she died on the table.

Barely hearing the other surgeon telling him that it was not his fault—that she would have died anyway, even had he not performed the risky operation—Trey Wentworth looked down at her lifeless body. He then stared at his hands, covered with her blood. The hands that had been so successful in dozens and dozens of operations had failed him now, when he needed them most.

Holding his hands up in front of him, he cried out in agony, "My god, what have I done? Her blood truly is on my hands. If I had not been so eager to try the new procedure, if I had not been so arrogant as to think I could do what dozens of other surgeons have not, she would still be alive. Then it would have been up to God, not me, whether she lived or died."

"You mustn't do this to yourself, Dr. Wentworth," his colleague insisted. "You let yourself get too close to the patient."

"I was going to marry her, Doctor," Trey retorted coldly. "She was my fiancée. How much closer could I get?" He looked down at the table and then picked up the lifeless hand of the young woman. "I'm sorry, Christine," he whispered in a choked voice, kissing the hand tenderly and then releasing it.

Turning his back on the operating table, he dropped his scalpel on the floor and walked away, determined never to pick up a surgical instrument again. He hurried out of the operating theater and closed the door firmly behind him, firmly closing the door on medicine as well.

———

Trey awakened with a start, and it took a few moments for him to realize where he was: riding the stagecoach to Buffalo, Wyoming, not walking the halls of Boston Mercy Hospital.

Dr. Caleb Alexander Wentworth had left the hospital and removed all his funds from the bank, and then he had gone to the railroad depot that very day, altering his name and taking the first train going west. Within weeks he had become a professional gambler, using his skilled hands to manipulate decks of cards rather than surgical tools and plying the saloons and gaming houses all over the West.

For the nearly ten years he had been out West, he had not communicated with anyone from his past. He had not sent so much as one word to any of his friends or colleagues back in Boston telling them he was alive or where he was or what he was doing.

Once, about a year ago, he was surprised to read an article about himself in a newspaper in Denver. "Whereabouts of noted surgeon still unknown," the headline had read. The story related how, after losing his betrothed on the operating table years before, Caleb Wentworth, M. D., had disappeared. According to the article, some people believed he had gone to Europe to practice medicine, while others believed they had spotted him on Boston's Skid Row. One person swore Trey had become a ship's surgeon, sailing the big windjammers to China. No one had guessed where he really was—or what he was doing.

The others in the coach all stirred awake as well, and as the gambler looked out at the eastern sky, he estimated that the sun had been up for nearly three hours. Just then he felt the coach begin to slow, and he glanced ahead and saw a man standing in the road, waving his arms to flag the stagecoach down.

———

On top of the coach, Dingo raised his shotgun, but Hank put out his hand to stop him. "Hold it," the driver ordered. "I recognize that young fella. That there is Clay Donovan. He's a friend of mine. Matter of fact, he used to drive for this company." Hank immediately hauled back on the reins and set the brake on the coach, bringing it to a halt.

Down on the road, Clay smiled broadly in recognition. "Hello, Hank," the escaped convict called. "It's good to see you."

"Well, Clay, I didn't know you was out of prison," Hank replied, grinning as well.

"I received a pardon," Clay lied.

"So what the hell are you doing out here on foot?" Hank asked. "Seems like a pretty foolish place to be."

"You're right. It is," Clay agreed, laughing. Running a hand through his sandy hair, he grinned sheepishly and explained, "Like a damned fool, I lost my horse and gear the other night. I've been wandering around ever since. Could you give me a lift?"

"I'd be glad to," Hank said. "I've got a full load, though. You'll have to ride on top."

"Suits me fine. The ride's better up there anyway," Clay quipped. He started toward the side of the coach when the door was suddenly opened, and Seth Reardon stepped out, his gun drawn.

"Hello, Clay," the lawman said, his experienced eyes assessing the young convict. "I heard about you breaking out of the penitentiary. I guess you know I'm gonna have to take your prisoner."

Clay sighed and then smiled. "Well, Seth, I reckon it's better than dying out here in the cold," he countered. He looked up at Hank. "Sorry about the lie, Hank. Seth's right. The truth is I escaped from prison about a week ago."

As the sheriff stepped in front of Clay and removed the revolver from his holster, the prisoner told him that it was empty. Seth then placed handcuffs on the young man's wrists.

Myron Haskell had been leaning out the window, watching what was happening, and he angrily leaped down from the coach, clutching the black satchel tightly to his chest. "Now, wait a minute! Just hold on here, Sheriff! You don't intend to bring that outlaw along with us, do you?" he blustered. "Especially in view of what we're carrying on this stage."

Clay squinted at Haskell and then asked, "That little black bag you're carrying there. It wouldn't happen to contain about one hundred thousand dollars, would it?"

Seth Reardon looked at his prisoner completely askance. "What the hell? Clay Donovan, how do you know about that?"

Clay grinned ruefully. "Well, the truth is I didn't just lose my horse. I had him shot from under me. You see, I broke out of prison hoping I could capture Brody Pike and force him to prove my innocence. I stumbled on his camp the other night and was sneaking around, trying to figure out how I could capture him, when I heard him telling his men that they'd soon have one hundred thousand dollars to divvy up. That's when I happened to kick loose a piece of shale and they got on to me. They chased me out of there and killed my animal, but I managed to get away in the dark—and here I am." He grinned, adding, "Pike wasn't none too specific about where the money was going to come from, but when this man started popping off, why I just put two and two together."

"Well, you came out with four all right," Seth confessed. "But what I'm wondering now is how did Pike find out about it?"

"I don't know, but if it's on this stage, he must be lying in wait up ahead," Clay suggested. Then he grinned again. "I guess that means I'm going to get another chance at him after all."

"Sheriff, I refuse to be a passenger or to allow the money I am carrying to be on the same stage with an escaped convict," Haskell grumbled.

"Well, I'm not leaving this man out here, Mr. Haskell," Seth replied, his voice impatient. "For one thing, it wouldn't be Christian. And for another, he's a wanted man and I'm a sheriff. I have to do my duty. So you've got no choice—unless *you* want to get out here and walk the rest of the way."

"It's a disgrace, an absolute disgrace," the bank clerk muttered. "If anything happens, I shall hold you personally responsible. That's a promise!"

Clay Donovan was about to climb up to the box when Seth motioned him toward the passenger compartment. "Clay, you'll ride inside where I can watch you better. There's no room on the seats, but you can ride on the floor."

Shrugging, Clay remarked, "Well, I'm not going to enjoy it as much, but I'll oblige you." So saying, he stepped inside, giving everyone a casual, sweeping glance. "Hello, folks, hope you don't mind the intru —" He stopped in midsentence at the sight of Rebecca McBride. "Rebecca," he gasped. "What...what are *you* doing here? I didn't think I'd ever see you again. I heard you had gone back east to finish school."

"Hello, Mr. Donovan," Rebecca replied coolly.

"'Mr. Donovan'?" the young man retorted. "It was never Mr. Donovan before."

Rebecca frowned at the handcuffs on Clay's wrists. "You were never a bank robber before," she countered.

"I'm not a bank robber now," he insisted.

"The court says you are."

"The court said the same thing about my brother," Clay said softly. "But I heard you were at his funeral, nevertheless."

"I could hardly do otherwise," the young woman said. "After all, Vince and I were engaged to be married."

"And tell me, Rebecca, when you were standing

there beside my brother's grave, did you really believe he had robbed a bank?"

Rebecca closed her eyes tightly, and tears trickled down her cheeks. She wiped them away quickly, almost angrily, and then turned and stared out the window.

When a moment or two had passed without her giving Clay an answer, he realized that none was coming.

On top of the coach, the driver whistled and shouted to his team. With a resounding crack of the whip, the stagecoach got underway again. "Answer me, girl," Clay almost shouted above the clacking wheels. "Did you really believe my brother robbed that bank?"

Rebecca turned and faced him. "No," she answered quietly.

"Then you can't believe that of me either. We were set up by Brody Pike."

"I know that's the story you told at your trial," the young woman said quietly.

"It was the truth, every word of it."

"Then why—" Rebecca began, but her voice broke slightly. Taking a deep breath, she went on, "Why didn't the jury believe you?"

"Maybe I can answer that question," Seth Reardon suggested. "I was at the trial, you may remember."

Smiling at the lawman, Clay told him, "I've never forgotten how you gave testimony on behalf of my brother and me. And I'm still grateful for your try."

"Yeah, well, I wish I could've done more. But to answer your question, Miss McBride, the reason the jury didn't believe him was because in a way it wasn't Clay Donovan who was on trial, it was the entire community of Banner."

Kate Langston looked at the lawman curiously. "What do you mean by that, Sheriff?" she asked.

"Well, when Brody Pike and his boys held up that bank, the whole town turned out to defend it," Seth explained. "But you may recall that Pike got away and one of the townspeople got killed. That made them even more determined to run Pike down and get revenge. So when they found Clay and Vince, why, they figured they had redeemed themselves some-what. Now, don't forget that the jury was made up of citizens from that same town, and they weren't about to deny the community its success. I don't think they intended to sentence an innocent man, I think they just refused to accept defeat—and if Clay had been proven innocent, in their eyes it would have been a defeat."

Kate looked down at Clay and told him kindly, "Well, I'd known you ever since you and Vince moved to the area and started your ranch, and if it means anything to you, I always thought you and your brother were innocent."

"Thank you, Mrs. Langston. It does indeed mean something to me."

"This is a lot of poppycock!" Myron Haskell fumed. "Sheriff, would you listen to yourself and the others? You're saying the only reason Donovan was found guilty was because he was tried in Banner. But if the people here are any indication, he would have been found innocent just by virtue of being tried in Buffalo! So nothing has been proven. The real test would be to try him somewhere other than Banner or Buffalo."

"That's just what I hoped to do by breaking out of prison," Clay remarked wryly. "I wanted to capture Brody Pike and then force another trial in a neutral location. I would be quite willing to accept the decision of that jury."

"Well, I am not from Banner or Buffalo, and were I to serve on a jury, I would find you guilty," the little clerk proclaimed.

"Without hearing the evidence?" Clay asked.

"Seeing you here in handcuffs is evidence enough for me," Haskell proclaimed. "You are an escaped criminal, and I intend to regard you as such." Facing the lawman, he added, "And what's more, Sheriff Reardon, I demand you do so as well. After all, you are a public servant, and I am carrying a great deal of money that is desperately needed by people in your own county. How do you think it would look to the ranchers there if the money they needed was lost because of your incompetence?"

Clearly trying to control his temper, the sheriff muttered, "Mr. Haskell, why don't you just relax and keep quiet? I'll see to it that the money gets through all right?"

Sitting on the floor of the coach with his back against the door and his knees drawn up before him, Clay looked up at Trey Wentworth and smiled. "I don't believe I've had the pleasure," he announced.

The gambler smiled down at him. "Trey. Trey Wentworth."

"I'm—"

"Clay Donovan. I know." Trey smiled. "Your reputation precedes you, Mr. Donovan."

"Call me Clay."

"Clay…" Tad Langston piped up, but his mother quickly shushed him.

"Tad, you are not to call an adult by his first name. You are to call him Mr. Donovan."

"But, Mama, he just said to call him Clay."

"He told *Mr. Wentworth* to call him Clay. Mr. Wentworth is an adult; you are a child."

Laughing, the prisoner declared, "I don't mind if he calls me Clay. Friends call each other by their first name, after all, and I'd like for Tad to be my friend. If it's all right with you, Mrs. Langston."

"Is it all right, Mama?"

Sighing, Kate conceded, "I suppose."

"Clay, I'm not feeling real good. Have you ever been sick?"

Clay looked from the boy to his mother and then back again. "Well, I sure have, and I'm sorry to hear that you're feeling poorly. But I'm sure you'll be better real soon."

After that, they rode in silence for a while, the passengers lost in their own thoughts. Several times Clay glanced up at Rebecca, sensing that she had been watching him from the corner of her eye. But each time he looked up, she glanced away, refusing to acknowledge him.

Clay had been very surprised to find Rebecca on this coach. If his life had not taken such an unexpected and tragic twist, Rebecca would have been his sister-in-law by now. He had often thought about that while he was in prison—about what it would have been like to have had the beautiful young woman married to his brother.

Would he have been able to remain on the ranch? To be that close to her and yet maintain a cool distance? What would he have done? How would he have lived with the fact that he was in love with his brother's wife?

It was that terrible secret that Clay Donovan carried with him. He had been silently and hopelessly in love with Rebecca McBride, his brother's fiancée.

Feeling a pang of guilt each time Clay glanced at her, Rebecca looked quickly away. Her heart was beating rapidly, and she hoped he would not notice the effect he had on her. Why did he have to show up now? She had closed the door to her past. She had buried Vince Donovan—literally—and with him, she thought, the terrible dilemma of being engaged to marry one man while being secretly in love with his brother.

She was not prepared to have the door to her past reopened, not even by so much as a crack, and she found herself wrestling with a tumult of emotions. A wild part of her, so deep inside her heart that she had never before realized that it existed, was ready to run away with him now. If he were to ask her, she would gladly forgo the wonders of Boston civilization and her own plans to take her father back with her. Willingly, she would run away with Clay Donovan to take whatever life had to offer, as long as they could face it together.

"No!" Rebecca cried.

"I beg your pardon, dear?" Kate asked.

Rebecca looked over at Kate. Realizing that she had spoken the word aloud, she felt her cheeks flush with her embarrassment, and it was as though her word still hung in the close atmosphere of the coach. She had been fighting so desperately against the wild dictates of her heart that the intensity of her battle had spilled from her lips without her having intended for it to do so.

"Oh," Rebecca finally said. "I'm sorry, Kate. I must've dozed off and talked in my sleep. My apologies."

Kate chuckled. "I understand, dear. It's been a tiring trip for all of us." She looked down at her son and brushed his red hair from his freckled face. "Tad's been so good," she said softly to Rebecca. "You know, I don't think that doctor did the least bit of good last night." She shook her head. "I might have more confidence if he had been sober."

"Mrs. Langston, his face appears flushed," Trey Wentworth suddenly observed. "Does he have a fever?"

Kate felt Tad's face and then nodded. "Yes," she answered. "Yes, he does." Taking the canteen from the floor, she wet her handkerchief and placed it on the boy's forehead. He looked up at her through pain-filled eyes.

Removing his own handkerchief from his pocket, Trey handed it to her. "Wet this one as well and put it on the back of his neck," he suggested. "It'll help bring the fever down."

"Thank you," Kate replied, smiling at the gambler.

She reached into her reticule. "I should probably give him another dose of this purgative—though it hasn't worked so far."

"May I see it?" Trey asked.

"Yes, of course," she replied, handing it to him.

Trey unstoppered the bottle, smelled it and then made a face and shook his head.

"I wouldn't give any more of this to your son if I were you," he advised.

Haskell looked over at Trey and snorted in distaste. "I hardly see where a man like you comes off telling the lady not to administer a curative that was prescribed by a doctor," he remarked.

"A drunken doctor," Kate pointed out in a sharp voice.

"But a doctor, nevertheless, madam. This man is nothing but a common gambler."

"That doesn't mean he can't have a gift for doctor-ing," Seth Reardon put it. "I've known lots of people with such a gift, and if they've got common sense and sober thought to go along with it, I'd say they're worth listening to as much as anybody."

Tad suddenly pleaded, "Mama, I don't want to take any more of that. It tastes horrible!" He had no sooner said the words that he leaped off Kate's lap, pushed his way to the window, and then stuck his head out. He gagged a few times, though nothing came up from his empty stomach. His face even paler than it was, Tad then climbed back onto his mother's lap.

Shaking her head, Kate Langston declared, "We'll

listen to Mr. Wentworth. You don't have to take any more."

Everyone fell silent again. Despite the discomfort, the rocking motion of the stagecoach lulled the passengers, and all of them—including Clay Donovan—soon fell asleep.

SIX

The stagecoach passengers had become accustomed to the long, tiring, bone-jarring ride, and throughout the rest of the day, they dozed frequently. Trey Wentworth managed to relieve some of the monotony of the waking hours of the journey by demonstrating card tricks for the others, and everyone was impressed by the dexterity of his hands and fingers—with the exception of Myron Haskell. The bank clerk made an obvious show of his total disdain for anything so trivial as card tricks, and he pointedly ignored the display, staring glumly out the window.

When the novelty of the card tricks had worn off, the passengers began exchanging stories. Seth Reardon, who had been a trooper in Custer's cavalry, told of the bloody massacre at the Little Bighorn. The lawman explained that he had been with Reno's troops, and he was therefore spared the fate that befell Custer and his men.

Kate Langston listened attentively and then added a little bit of information that the sheriff had omitted. "He's much too modest a man to tell this part of it," she explained, "and I wouldn't have known myself had a visiting Army officer not informed me one day. You see, Seth was awarded the Medal of Honor for his part in that battle."

"The Medal of Honor!" Trey exclaimed. "Well, Sheriff, I am very impressed."

"All I did was get a little water for some of my comrades," Seth mumbled. "It hardly seemed like something to get the medal for. Still," he added, a faraway look on his face, "it was a proud moment when President Grant pinned it on me."

When it was Kate's turn to entertain the others, she told a story of the night Bat Masterson had stayed at her hotel and then had a gunfight before breakfast the next morning. "It was over so fast that I wasn't even certain I saw it happen," she quipped. "A jump of the shoulder, a loud pop, a cloud of smoke, and a man lay dead in the street while Bat Masterson stood over him, a smoking gun in his hand."

"I remember that," Seth put in. "I was a deputy then."

"Did you attempt to arrest him?" Trey asked.

"There was no reason to. There were more than a dozen witnesses to the incident, including Mrs. Langston here, and they all swore that the man drew on Masterson without any provocation."

"I was out on the ranch when he came into Buffalo," Rebecca McBride recalled. "Papa wouldn't even let me come into town to see him—although I was very curious. What did he look like?"

"Oh, he was quite the handsome peacock," Kate said, chuckling. "He had coal-black hair and slate-blue eyes. But what really made him stand out was the way he dressed." Kate smiled. "He was what you might call a fancy-Dan dresser." She then glanced at Trey Wentworth, as if suddenly aware of the similarity of clothing. Their eyes met, and he smiled, but she quickly looked away, embarrassed.

Rebecca then shared with the others some of the wonders she had encountered in Boston—such things as the telephone, electric lights, elevators, and magic-lantern shows.

"I was reminded of all the mean tricks I've seen our cowboys pull on the dudes from the East," she said, giggling, "For I was a 'rube' from out West and as fair game for their jokes as any tenderfoot ever was for a bit of western fun. Once, when we were painting one of the rooms of the dormitory, the other girls sent me to a store to buy some spotted paint."

The others in the coach laughed.

"I know, I know," Rebecca agreed, "it sounds perfectly ridiculous to think I would fall for something like that. But you must remember, my mind had been bedazzled with all the inventions of modern society— inventions we had never even heard of out here, much less seen. I was perfectly willing to believe that there was such a thing as spotted paint."

Clay was next in the line of storytellers, and he soon was regaling everyone with a hilarious story of some of the antics of his fellow prisoners.

When everyone had fallen silent, Rebecca asked the gambler, "What about you, Mr. Wentworth? Do you have a story you could share with us?"

Trey looked thoughtful for a moment and then told about a balloon ascension he had once made in France. "I went aloft with the celebrated aeronaut Gaston Tissandier," he told the others. "It was a most exciting excursion, and I was given the job of monitoring the other passengers for oxygen deprivation, while of course making certain that I didn't get into trouble myself.

"As we got to fourteen thousand feet, we all began to get a little giddy. From there on up, I insisted that we use the oxygen in greater and greater doses. Then disaster struck. The gas-relief valve froze on the balloon, and for a while we were afraid we would keep going up and up without stop. Then suddenly—and fortunately—the balloon burst, and our descent was assured...although it was at a far more rapid rate than we would have wished," he concluded wryly.

"How was it you weren't killed?" Kate asked, on the edge of her seat from the excitement and tension of the story.

"When the gas bag exploded, it formed a huge, inverted cup, much like an umbrella," Trey explained. "Consequently, it set us down as gently as a feather."

"My, what a marvelous adventure!" Kate declared, her eyes shining with pleasure, and the others added their own words of appreciation for his story.

"Poppycock!" Haskell scoffed. "You might have the others convinced, Wentworth, but not me. What would a gambler being doing in France?"

"I haven't always been a gambler, Mr. Haskell," Trey said. "You, on the other hand, have probably always been a jackass."

Trey's comment brought an outburst of laughter from the others in the coach. Myron Haskell merely clutched his black satchel to his chest even more tightly while he fumed in silence.

Shortly after that the coach stopped, and Seth Reardon leaned out the window, a slight breeze ruffling his hair. "I wonder why we're stopping here," he asked rhetorically as he pulled his head back inside. "This isn't the way station."

"Sheriff?" Hank Bailey called down from up top on the driver's seat. "Sheriff, you want to come out of the coach for a minute?"

"Sure thing," Seth replied, opening the door and stepping outside. He walked a few steps forward and then looked up at Hank, who was standing on his seat and pointing toward a small cluster of buildings about a quarter of a mile ahead.

"As you know, that there's Powder River Station," the driver said. "We're supposed to change teams and spend the night there—but I don't know. I don't like the looks of it. I don't see no smoke nor nothin'. It just don't appear to be right."

Shading his eyes, the lawman looked ahead. Finally, shaking his head, he suggested, "Well, we aren't going to find out anything by staying here, so you may as well drive on in. But be real careful."

"Hey, Sheriff," Dingo called, his weathered face screwed up with concern, "are you any good with a long gun?"

"I reckon I can hit what I'm aiming at," Seth answered laconically. "Why do you ask?"

"Well, sir, besides this here shotgun I'm carryin', I got two Winchesters up here in the boot. I'd be obliged iffen you'd take one of 'em and come up on top till we get into the station."

Nodding in agreement, Hank added, "Yeah, as a matter of fact, I believe I'd appreciate that myself, if you don't mind."

"All right," Seth answered.

"Sheriff, what's wrong?" Myron Haskell called, sticking his head out the window. "What's going on?"

"Mr. Haskell, you and the others just stay put inside," Seth answered. "I'm going to ride on top of the coach until we get into the station."

"What about this escaped criminal we have in here?" Haskell asked in a disbelieving, reproving voice. "Are you just going to leave him in the coach with us? We are unarmed and helpless. If he decides to try something, who will protect us from him?"

"Don't be afraid of him, Haskell. You've got Tad and the ladies to watch out for you," Seth countered.

The others laughed appreciatively at the remark, which only served to rile the banker more. "See here, Sheriff! This is no laughing matter," Haskell said angrily. "I demand you do something about this prisoner."

"Mr. Haskell, you certainly are one for making demands," Seth said. Sighing, he said, "All right, Clay, why don't you climb up on top with me?"

"Suits me," Clay agreed easily. Exiting the coach, he climbed up to the luggage rack and then sat down and leaned back against the trunks. Seth climbed up alongside him and then took one of the rifles from Dingo.

"All right, Hank," the lawman said, "you drive her on in and let's see what we can find out."

Nodding, the driver nudged his shotgunner. "Dingo, you keep your eyes open. If you see anythin', you let me know and I'll snap a whip over these critters so fast, they'll think they're gettin' ready to run that there Kentucky Derby."

A few minutes later the coach pulled into the depot. Halfway between the corral and the main building, a man was lying unmoving on his stomach.

"That there is Levi Powell," Hank announced softly, pointing to the body as he halted the team. "He's one of the hostlers here."

Just then the door opened on the coach, and Seth Reardon ordered sharply, "Stay inside the coach! All of you!"

Trey Wentworth called back, "Sheriff, I'd just like to take a closer look at that man over there, if you don't mind. Perhaps he's still alive."

Weighing the idea for a moment, the lawman relented. "All right, I reckon you can take a look if you want to. I'm pretty damn sure there's nothing you're gonna be able to do for him, though."

Stepping out of the coach, Trey walked over to the body. Squatting down behind him, he put his hand on the man's cheeks to test his body temperature. He then moved the hostler's arms and legs to test the degree of rigor mortis.

Turning to the driver, Seth asked Hank, "See

anything?" Both the driver and the shotgunner were standing on top of the stage, sweeping the area carefully with their gazes.

"No, I don't see nothin'," Hank replied. "How about you, Dingo?"

"No, I don't see nothin' either. Maybe I'll just climb down and take a look around," he volunteered and then flicked a glance at the lawman. "If that's all right with you, Sheriff."

"Yeah, sure. Go ahead," Seth replied, never taking his eyes from the scene.

Dingo hopped down from the coach and began looking around the station. It was quiet—so quiet that the silence itself became a presence. That was particularly evident when the windmill behind the one-story log building responded to a breeze and suddenly swung around with a loud squeaking clank and then started spinning.

Like the others, Seth was startled by the sudden sound, and he swung his rifle toward the stable, only to see the windmill whirling into life.

Clay Donovan then stepped down from the coach and looked up at the lawman. "Sheriff, have you noticed that there are no horses in the stable?" he mentioned, motioning toward the corral.

"Yeah," Seth answered. "I noticed that."

Dingo had neared the front porch of the main building when he suddenly stopped. He stared for a moment and then came back to the coach, walking back at a much quicker pace.

"What is it?" Hank asked. "What did you find?"

"There's two more bodies over there," he said,

pointing. "I think one of 'em might be the stationmaster. Both of 'em's been shot."

Seth rubbed his chin thoughtfully and then asked, "What do you think, Dingo? Is this the work of Indians?"

"No, I don't think so," the shotgun guard answered, scratching his sparsely covered head. "Leastwise, whoever done this sure ain't acted like no Indians I've ever seen. All of 'em was shot, and there's no scalpin' and no knife wounds."

"Well, whoever it was, I don't think they're around here anymore," Hank offered. "I mean, it seems too damn quiet for that."

Trey came back to the stage and looked up at Seth. "If it means anything, that man over there hasn't been dead for more than three or four hours," he said.

Nodding, Seth responded, "It probably means that whoever did this has been gone that long."

"In that case, is it all right to let my passengers out?" Hank asked. "I hope you ain't plannin' on keepin' these folks in the coach forever," he went on. "They got to be able to get out and stretch their legs a bit. Especially the ladies."

"Yeah," Seth said. "I know what you mean. But, before we let them out, let me check the outhouses, just to make certain there are no unpleasant surprises waiting inside. In the meantime, Dingo, you want to get a tarp or something over those bodies?"

"I'll do better'n that, Sheriff," Dingo offered, starting back toward the barn. "There's gotta be some shovels kept back in the barn. I'll get 'em buried."

Seth Reardon watched Dingo's retreating back for a

moment, and then he hopped down and made a thorough check of the area. Coming back to the stagecoach, he opened the door to the coach, telling the passengers, "All right, folks, it seems safe enough. You can come on out now, if you want to."

"Thanks," Kate Langston said, brushing back a stray lock of her auburn hair, which was glistening with sweat. "I don't think I could have stayed in this coach for another minute."

As the passengers wandered around the station, Hank and Dingo dug graves for the three dead men. "We'll leave a letter for the next coach that comes through here, tellin' what we did," Hank explained to Seth. "I don't want to take them poor fellas on the stage with us, but there's no way we can just leave 'em lyin' out here."

"I agree," the lawman said.

Coming alongside the men, Kate Langston looked at Hank and asked, "Mr. Bailey, would it be all right if I look around the kitchen? Perhaps I can find something to fix for our supper."

"I think that would be a grand idea, ma'am," Hank answered. "I hadn't thought of it, but now that you mention it, I am mighty hungry."

"Kate, would you like some help?" Rebecca McBride offered.

"I'd love some help," Kate replied. The redhead then put her arm protectively around her son's shoulders. "Come along, Tad. You stay inside with us, out of everyone's way."

Myron Haskell was sitting on the boarding step of the coach, an annoyed expression on his face. When

Seth Reardon neared, the bank clerk pointed over toward Clay Donovan, who was wandering around the yard, examining the tracks that had been left in the dirt. "Sheriff," the little man asked, "are you just going to let your prisoner roam around free like that?"

"What do you mean, free?" Seth replied. "Can't you see that his hands are manacled?"

"That isn't enough," Haskell countered. "He should be chained to a tree or to the wheel of the stage or something. He shouldn't be allowed to roam around like that. For all we know, it might have been him that killed all these people here. You are placing every passenger on this coach in jeopardy."

Sighing impatiently, the lawman stared at the man. "Haskell, you aren't seriously trying to blame these killings on Donovan, are you? How in the hell could he have done them? He was with us."

"He wasn't with us last night. He joined us this morning, if you remember," Haskell remarked stiffly. "Who is to say he didn't do this during the night and then ride away from the scene of the crime? Perhaps his horse went lame along the way, and that was why he was out on the trail looking for a ride. Or he could even be riding with us to establish his alibi."

"Come on, Haskell, you're not making any sense! You heard what Mr. Wentworth said. These men have been dead no more than three or four hours. That means Clay couldn't have done it."

"Do you mean to say you are going to take a gambler's word on how long these unfortunate victims have been dead?" Haskell asked scornfully.

"Why not?" Seth snapped. "His guess seems as good as anyone else's."

"Nevertheless, I am making a note of this," the clerk promised, "along with the several other errors in judgment I have seen you make. And I will hold you accountable for them."

"You just go ahead and do that, Haskell," Seth retorted with disgust.

A heavy silence fell, which was broken when Clay called, "Sheriff, you want to come over here and take a look at this?"

More than willing to oblige, Seth walked over to where Clay was standing.

"Mr. Haskell still giving you trouble, is he?" Clay asked dryly, giving the fastidious little man a sidelong glance.

"He's trying to," Seth admitted. "But never mind him. What have you found?"

Raising his manacled hands, Clay pointed to some hoofprints in the dirt. "You see this tie-bar shoe?" he asked. "While I was sneaking around Brody Pike's camp, I noticed that one of their horses was shod this way." He gestured toward the main building, adding, "This is Brody Pike's work."

"Brody Pike, huh?" Seth said. "Yeah, I was afraid of that. And if they know about the money, that means they're after us. But what gets me is why did they have to kill everyone here?"

"I imagine they wanted to run the horses away so they could keep us from having a fresh team," Clay answered. "That would sure give them an advantage —and the only way they could do that would be to kill the men who work here." Shrugging, he added, "I suppose the only reason they didn't stick around and attack us here is they were afraid some other coaches might come along as well."

"That means they're going to be waiting up ahead, aren't they?" Seth asked.

Nodding, the prisoner replied, "That's my guess. So, what are you going to do?"

"Well, I reckon I'm gonna have to give this a little thought," the lawman answered, shaking his head. Folding his arms across his broad, muscular chest, Seth Reardon stared into the distance, his eyes unfocused, as he considered their dilemma.

By the time the bodies were buried and the horses watered and fed, Rebecca came out to announce that supper, which consisted of fried salt pork, biscuits, and gravy, was ready.

"Sorry about the fare, gentlemen, but this is all we could find," Kate Langston apologized as the men filed inside the station building.

"It smells awfully good to me," Clay remarked, and the others concurred.

As they all sat down around the table, Seth Reardon called for their attention. When everyone quieted down, he told them, "I'd like to talk some things over with you folks. Judging from the tracks that Clay spotted, it's more'n likely that Brody Pike and his bunch were the ones who murdered the men here, meaning it's likely that they know about the money. And it's possible that they're figuring on hitting us tonight, while we're asleep. I think we should go on—even though there's a damn good chance that they'll be waiting up ahead for us."

Hank swallowed a chunk of biscuit and then pointed out, "The problem with goin' on, though, means we're gonna have to take this same team right back out without a rest after they've been workin' all day."

"I'm afraid that can't be helped," Seth responded. "I think it's too dangerous to stay here…especially with the ladies and the boy."

"We could maybe head on over to Antelope Springs and put the ladies off there," the driver suggested.

"No! I'm going on," Rebecca McBride said. She smiled sheepishly at the forcefulness of her remark and then added, "I mean, I didn't want to leave Boston in the first place, but I did. And now that I've come this far, I don't intend to be put off by the likes of Brody Pike."

"I agree with Rebecca," Kate agreed. She put a plate of food in front of her son, her expression encouraging, but Tad merely looked at it listlessly. "I've come too far to stop now." She laid the back of her hand on her son's freckled face. "Besides, I want to get Tad to Dr. Colburn as quickly as I can."

"I, too, feel we should go on," Myron Haskell agreed.

"Well, there's a switch," Seth remarked dryly, an amused expression on his face. "I was sure you would want us to turn around and go back."

Giving the lawman a look of disdain, the bank clerk said huffily, "I have an obligation to the people who are waiting for this money. Regardless of what you may think of me, Sheriff, I am a banker, and I hold that responsibility very seriously."

Shrugging, the sheriff looked at the gambler. "Mr. Wentworth, how about you?"

"Whatever the others want is fine with me," Trey said. "I have no preference one way or the other."

"All right, then. We'll push on ahead."

"I have a suggestion, Seth," Clay Donovan offered.

"Let's hear it."

Laying down his fork, the young rancher ran his finger along the right side of it to illustrate his point and suggested, "The regular stage road goes along the east side of these mountains, along the Powder River. Instead of taking it, why don't we go up Willow Creek?" Shifting his manacled hands, he moved his finger along the opposite side of the fork. "That's on the west side. Pike and his gang won't be looking for us there."

"I don't know," Seth replied slowly, rubbing his stubbly chin as he pondered the idea. "I've been that way on horseback a couple of times. Some of that country is mighty rough. And frankly, I don't know if we could get the stage through that way."

"I remember a wagon trail that the miners used to use," Clay said. "We can take the stage anywhere they could take their wagons."

"It's possible, I suppose," the lawman murmured. Turning to the driver, he asked, "What do you think, Hank?"

"I can't rightly say for sure," Hank answered as he studied Clay's fork over the rim of his cup. "Clay's correct about one thing, though. There is a wagon route that goes up the west side." He paused for a moment and took a sip of his coffee; then he went on, "It'd be hard goin', but I think it could be done."

"There's a problem ain't neither one of you is considerin'," Dingo pointed out, the words somewhat muffled by the food in his mouth.

"What's that?"

"Well, we ain't changin' the team *here*, so that means that if we go up the west side, we ain't gonna be able to change the team for the whole rest of the way. The coach can maybe make it through the trail, but the problem is, can the horses make it? They may get so plumb tuckered out that they just drop, right in their harness."

"Not if we baby them as much as possible," Clay suggested. "We can leave all the luggage here, locked in the storeroom, and send a wagon back for it later. We'll take only a few necessities—including whatever food and cooking utensils we can rustle up here. And when we have a pretty steep grade, all the passengers could help things along by getting out and walking."

"It might work," Hank admitted.

"Wait a minute! Hold on here!" Myron Haskell said. "I'm against all this!"

"I thought you were wanting to go on ahead," Seth said, looking at the man through narrowed eyes.

"Yes, I did, as long as we were going to go by the regular route," Haskell replied. "But this man is a known outlaw. I mean, what do we know about him? He suddenly appeared on the trail this morning, telling us he was set afoot by Brody Pike. Well, I don't believe him. I think it's likely that he's in with that gang of thieves and cutthroats, and now he's just trying to set us up for an ambush. If we go on the west side of the mountains, there won't be anyone we can turn to for help."

Seth Reardon stared at the stiff little man. "If Pike and his bunch hit us out there on the trail, there won't be anyone we can turn to for help, no matter *which* side of the mountain we're on," the lawman said. "And if they're looking for us on the east side, then the west side is our best bet."

"Unless, of course, this man has arranged for Pike to be there."

Sighing impatiently, Seth remarked, "I've known Clay for a long time. Like I said before, I believed him at his trial when he said he was set up by Brody Pike, and I believe him now when he says he overheard them making plans. And I *don't* believe he would try and set the rest of us up for an ambush. He's not the kind of man that could do something like that." Throwing up his hands, he added, "But the decision isn't mine to make. Hank, you're the driver. What do you say?"

"Well, I tell you, Seth, I've known Clay about as long as you have, and I don't believe he's in with that bunch either. And since Pike is most likely waitin' for us up along the Powder River Road somewhere, then I think we should go up Willow Creek."

"Dingo?"

"I'm paid to ride shotgun, Sheriff, not make no decisions," Dingo replied as he broke open two more biscuits and covered them with gravy. "You want to take this here coach to China, well, I reckon I'll be sittin' up there on the box the whole way…long as I get paid." He shrugged, stating, "Go whichever way you want to. It don't make me no never mind."

"Sheriff, may I raise a concern?" Trey asked.

"Go ahead."

"You're a lawman, and if you believe Mr. Donovan is telling the truth, then I certainly have no reason to doubt it. But in case you have forgotten, we have a sick boy with us. He needs to get to Buffalo as quickly as possible. Now, which way is faster?"

"The Powder River route is faster by at least half a day, maybe more," Hank replied.

"Then, for the boy's sake, perhaps we should take that route…or at least give his mother the option of being the deciding factor."

"Mrs. Langston," Seth asked. "Do you want us to keep going home this way?"

"No," Kate answered emphatically. "You remember that horrible incident about a year ago, when they found a rancher, his wife, and their little girl and little boy murdered? Everyone knows Brody Pike is the one who did it. It might mean Tad being sick for a bit longer before he sees the doctor, but I'd rather him be sick than dead." She shuddered slightly, adding, "And if Brody Pike finds us, I'm afraid that's what we'll all be."

"Then it's decided," Seth announced. "We'll go by way of the Willow Creek wagon road."

"Dingo," Hank said, wiping his mouth and getting up from the table. "What say you and me go outside and start unloadin' the stagecoach? We need to get it as light as we can."

"Anybody gonna eat this last biscuit an' piece of meat?" Dingo asked, pointing at the platter. When no one answered, he made a sandwich and then took a bite of it as he quickly followed Hank out the door.

Seth then stood and walked around to Clay. "We won't be needin' these things anymore," he said, unlocking Clay's handcuffs.

"What?" Myron Haskell sputtered angrily. "Just what do you think you're doing?"

"If Brody Pike figures out what we're doing and comes after us, we're gonna need every gun we've got," the lawman replied.

"Sheriff! You don't seriously intend to—"

"I certainly do intend," the lawman interjected, cutting Haskell off. Drawing himself up to his full, commanding height, he asked sharply, "Does anyone else object?"

"The more guns we have, the safer I'll feel," Kate Langston agreed.

"You'll certainly get no objections from me," Trey added.

Rebecca McBride was watching the young prisoner with admiration. "Nor from me. I trust Clay completely."

Smiling, Clay promised the young woman, "You won't be sorry."

Angrily, Haskell stormed out of the building, slamming the door behind him.

"You're going to need this as well," Seth told the young man, handing Clay his revolver.

"With bullets?"

Seth smiled. "Oh, yes. You did tell me it was empty, didn't you. He shoved a dozen slugs out of his gun belt and handed them over. Clay pushed six of them into empty shots on his own belt and then loaded the other six into the cylinder of his pistol.

"Dingo tells me there's an extra rifle, too," Seth said.

His blue eyes regarding the lawman intently, Clay smiled and replied softly, "Thanks, Seth. I won't betray your trust."

"I know you won't."

SEVEN

I t had been a long time since the mining road
had been used, and the route, though passable,
was extremely difficult. At one point, the stage
lurched so sharply to the left that everyone inside was
thrown against each other or the sides of the stagecoach. Tad Langston cried out in pain, and Kate
comforted him as best she could, although her eyes
betrayed her concern.

"We were fools, absolute fools to come this way!"
Myron Haskell yelled.

"We all agreed that this was the way we were
going to come, Mr. Haskell," Rebecca McBride pointed
out.

"No, we did *not* all agree. I never consented to this
decision."

"You got on the coach, Mr. Haskell," Seth Reardon
reminded the clerk, his clear blue eyes boring into
him. "By that action, you agreed."

"Whoa!" Hank Bailey suddenly shouted from his seat on the box, and the coach came to an abrupt halt.

"Now what?" Haskell asked.

Clay Donovan, who had been riding on top of the coach, climbed down, and dropped to the ground. Opening the door, he announced, "Folks, I'm afraid you're all going to have to get out and walk a bit. There's a pretty steep grade coming up, and we're going to need to lighten the coach."

Trey Wentworth stepped out of the coach first. Turning to help the others, he held out his hand to prevent Tad from getting out when the boy appeared in the doorway. "I think it would be best if you stayed in the coach, son," he told him kindly. "You don't weigh enough to make that much difference and you shouldn't be walking."

"Do you think that would be all right, Clay?" Kate asked, poking her head out the doorway over her son's shoulder.

"Sure," Clay replied. "Trey's right. He doesn't need to walk."

"I can walk," Tad insisted. "I'm not a baby."

"I know you're not a baby, Tad," Clay replied kindly. "That's why I think you could do something for me, if you would."

"What?"

"Well, somebody has to stay inside and keep an eye on things for us in there. Since you weigh the least, I was sort of hoping you would do it. You can even lie down while you're doing it."

"Oh. Sure, all right," Tad agreed. His face was pale,

and his eyes were slightly glazed as he moved back into the coach and lay back down.

When Haskell got out, he looked up at the driver's seat where Hank sat holding the reins. "Mr. Bailey, just so that you fully understand, I want you to know that I shall be writing a letter to the Wyoming Express Company, demanding a refund of my fare. I paid to *ride* to Buffalo, not walk."

"Yes, sir," Hank replied. "I'm sure you'll be writin' to the company with all kinds of complaints. From what I can tell, you don't ever seem to run out of 'em."

"And I'll add surliness to my list of complaints as well," Haskell promised, shaking his finger angrily. "There's no excuse for you to be discourteous to your passengers."

"I reckon not." His voice amused, Hank said, "Now, if I ask you real polite, would you please walk in back of the coach along with all the other passengers?"

Sniffing derisively, the bank clerk did as he was asked, clutching his satchel protectively to his thin chest.

With everyone walking along behind the coach, the driver whistled to the team, and they started up the grade. It was a long, gradual climb, and the coach moved no faster than the passengers were walking. When they finally reached the top of the hill, Hank gave the horses a few minutes to rest, and then he informed the passengers they could re-board.

It was late enough in the day now that the western sky was ablaze with color. Rebecca McBride was watching the sunset through the window on her side of the coach, and she exclaimed to her friend, "Oh, Kate, would you look at that beautiful sky? How could I have ever let the loveliness of these sunsets, the beauty of this wild, rugged country, slip away from me? Boston has much to offer, I'll admit—but it has nothing to compare with all this."

Kate chuckled. "Is this the same Rebecca McBride who was on the train with me? The young woman who was so resentful of having been brought back and who could hardly wait to convince her father that the only sensible thing to do was sell his ranch and move to Boston?"

"There have been a few changes in the way I look at things since then," Rebecca admitted, her face flushing slightly.

Kate reached over and squeezed her hand. "I'm glad to hear that," she said. "You and your pa are real good people, Rebecca, and if Wyoming ever becomes a state, it's going to be because we have a lot of people like you and your pa out here."

The coach hit another bump at that moment, and Tad make a sharp little cry.

The redhead immediately became solicitous of her son, saying, "Oh, Tad, honey, I wish I could make the hurt go away."

"Mrs. Langston," Trey said quietly, "perhaps the boy would be more comfortable if you undid the top buttons of his trousers and loosened them. That would take some of the pressure off his stomach."

"Yes," Kate agreed. "Yes, I'm sure that's a good idea. I hadn't thought of that." She started to unbutton

Tad's pants, but the boy put his hand down to stop her.

"No, Mama," he complained. "If you do that, when I walk, my pants will fall down, and people will laugh at me."

"Honey, you heard what Clay said. He wants you to stay in the coach and keep an eye on things. You aren't going to have to walk anywhere," Kate reminded him.

"And besides, if anyone happened to laugh at you, I'd put 'em in jail," Seth offered.

"You promise?"

"I promise."

"All right," Tad agreed, nodding solemnly. "You can unbutton them, Mama."

"How does your stomach feel now, Tad?" Trey asked, his concern evident.

"That does make it feel better," Tad told him. "But it still hurts somethin' awful."

Kate smoothed back the boy's hair and promised, "We'll soon have you at Dr. Colburn's. Then you'll be fine."

Listening to the conversations inside the coach from his seat on the roof, Clay Donovan thought that what he had missed most being in prison were the little things that everyone takes for granted when they have their freedom. He had almost forgotten how pleasurable it was just to have a quiet talk with a good friend—without having a guard watching, thinking you were planning something. How he had missed walking in the woods, feeling the springy softness of pine needles underfoot while listening to the song of some bird. Or the simple pleasure gotten from sitting on a porch swing, moving lazily, while watching a sunset.

Yeah, he thought to himself, *I've forgotten what normalcy feels like as opposed to the artificial existence of being in a cage.*

When the coach had to be emptied again a half hour later, Clay hopped down and walked directly behind the coach. Rebecca McBride dawdled about ten yards behind the others, taking in the beauty of the mountains. Clay's heart began to pound as he watched the beautiful young woman, and he dropped back to walk alongside her.

"I can't tell you how good it is to see you again," he told her, keeping her pace.

"Why?" she asked.

"Why? Well, because...because you were my brother's fiancée," he told her, shrugging. "And I wanted to make certain that you understood that Vince and I didn't do what they said we did."

"I guess I never believed that you did," Rebecca admitted, looking down at her feet.

"You didn't?"

"No."

"But you went away. You left to go to school in Boston."

"Yes, that's true—although actually it was my father's idea, but I went along with it. You have to understand that there was nothing left for me here. I... I couldn't bear to ride by your ranch every day... seeing all the work that you and Vince did and knowing how close the two of you were to your dream

—only to see it going to waste. Vince was dead, you were in prison and...and I felt empty inside."

"I do understand that," Clay murmured.

"Was it...was it awful in prison?"

Clay smiled wryly. "Well, the whole idea of a prison is to make it a place that a person never wants to see again," he explained. "The hope is that after such an unpleasant experience, a man will reform when he gets out rather than do something that will send him back."

"Does it work?"

"I don't think so," Clay answered, sighing. "In fact, I think it just makes most men harder. I'm not saying people like Brody Pike don't deserve to go to prison— or hang, for that matter—I'm just saying that the experience inside a prison generally makes a man worse than he was when he went in."

"But it didn't make you worse," Rebecca offered, touching Clay's arm briefly. "You are as sweet now as you were when you were going to be my brother-in-law."

Clay looked intently at Rebecca, searching her face. "You know, that wasn't something I was looking forward to," he confessed.

"You mean you didn't want to be my brother-in-law?"

"No."

"Why not?" she asked lightly. "What are you trying to do, hurt my feelings?"

"No," Clay said softly. "I was trying to keep from hurting Vince."

"I don't understand."

Taking a deep breath, Clay told her, "I'm afraid I never really thought of you as a sister-in-law. I had other, more personal thoughts than that—thoughts that I didn't think I could share with anyone."

"Oh!" Rebecca exclaimed, and her face changed abruptly. For a fleeting moment, her face held a look of pure delight. Then, just as quickly, it clouded over, and she shook her head fiercely. "Clay, you really shouldn't —" Rebecca began, but Clay put his hand out to stop her.

"No, wait, let me speak," he insisted. "Vince is dead now, and he has been for two years. I never said anything about this before because it wasn't my place. You were engaged to Vince and I wouldn't do anything to hurt you or him. When I was in prison, I was in no position to even let myself think about such things, let alone say them. But now there's no one left who could be hurt, and there's no reason—"

"No, don't say it!" Rebecca begged, interrupting him. "Please, Clay, don't say it!"

Puzzled, he muttered, "You don't know what I'm going to say."

Rebecca looked up at him through tear-filled yes. "Yes, I do know," she half-whispered. "You are going to tell me that you love me."

He stared at her, surprised. "But how could you know? I've never said anything about it before…I've never so much as breathed a word about it."

"Nevertheless, I know," Rebecca said, looking away. "And the reason I know is because I feel the same way about you." She then gazed at him again, her face beseeching. "But we couldn't speak of it then, Clay, and we can't now. Don't you see? We must not."

"Rebecca!" Clay blurted, barely hearing her last words. "Did you mean what you just said? Could it be true that you love me?"

"Please, Clay, don't make me say it. I beg of you."

Clay suddenly reached for her, but she broke away from him and ran to the stage. Then she walked quickly around to the opposite side of the coach so that he could not see her, and he knew that she wanted to regain her composure.

Clay was as puzzled by what he felt was her odd behavior as he was elated that she felt about him the way he did about her. It took all his willpower to keep from rushing to her to take her in his arms and kiss her, telling her that everything would be all right. But he knew that at that moment she was like a frightened bird, and the best thing he could do would be not to frighten her more. Reluctantly, he did not pursue her.

When they reached the top of the grade, Hank Bailey let the horses rest again. By now the sun was just below the horizon, and the red of the sunset was turning purple, while the purple was already turning to black. It would be dark before much longer, and the passengers had already decided that they were not going to try to push through the night. However, Hank did have a particular place in mind where he wanted to make camp, and that was another five miles or so. There, Hank told them, they could find water and as it was in a little valley, they would be able to have some shelter from the cold night wind.

Dingo was tending to the horses and seeing him

standing alone near the head of the team, Clay walked up to him. He had been looking for the opportunity to speak with the shotgunner alone, and now he looked around to make certain no one was close enough to overhear them.

"Where were you in prison, Dingo?" he asked without preamble.

Surprised, Dingo gasped and looked up at him sharply. "Who told you I was ever in prison?" he demanded.

"You did."

"Me? Why, I never did no such thing! What makes you say I told you?"

"There's a look a person gets when he's inside," Clay explained. "That look never goes away, no matter how long ago it was. You have that look, my friend."

Dingo was quiet for a long moment; then he glanced back at the others. Finally he let out a long sigh. "Yeah," he said. "I reckon I do know about that look. Please don't say nothin' about it, Clay. Nobody else knows, and if the company found out, I'd most likely lose my job. I can't see the Wyoming Express Company hirin' a man who once served time for robbin' a stage. And it's awful hard tryin' to go straight if you ain't got no job."

"I surely do see your point," Clay replied. "When were you in?"

"About five years ago," Dingo answered, fingering the scar on his face.

"Here in Wyoming?"

"No. It was back in Kansas."

"Kansas?" Clay echoed. "Brody Pike was in state prison there about five years ago, wasn't he?"

Dingo's eyes narrowed, and he nodded cautiously.

"You met him there, didn't you?" Clay guessed.

Looking at him warily, Dingo replied, "Yeah. Fact is, Brody Pike was my cellmate."

———

While the others took the opportunity to leave the wagon road and go into the surrounding woods to refresh themselves, Trey Wentworth walked over to talk to Kate Langston, who was looking in through the coach window at her son.

"Are you doing all right?" he asked, gauging her carefully.

"Yes, I'm doing just fine, thank you," Kate answered, smiling at him. She nodded toward the inside of the stage. "I wish I could say the same for Tad, poor thing."

"Is he sleeping now?"

"Yes."

"Well, that's the best thing for him at the moment," Trey advised. "If he's asleep, he's totally relaxed, and the more relaxed he is, the less strain he puts on his stomach muscles—hence the less pain he's going to feel." Sticking his hand in through the open window, he felt Tad's face. "He's still fevered," he said, "although, for the moment, it doesn't seem to be out of hand."

She cocked her head and stared at him for a long

moment, then said, "Seth is right. You really do have a feel for doctoring, don't you?"

"Well, I thought I did…once," the gambler answered without elaboration.

"Maybe you should be a doctor."

Trey smiled at her sadly. "No, I'm afraid I can't agree with you there."

They were both silent for a moment, and then Trey said, "Tell me about this man in Buffalo, your doctor there. I believe you said his name was Dr. Colburn?"

"Yes, Wesley Colburn. He's an older man who has experienced just about everything. He's certainly done his share of removing bullets and arrows and repairing broken bones and such. I believe he's a very good doctor, and he's pulled a lot of folks through some pretty bad times."

"Do you have faith in him?"

"Yes." Kate got a distant look in her eyes before continuing. "He wasn't able to save my husband, but I'm convinced that he did everything he could. Yes, I'd say that I have faith in him."

"Then that's the most important thing," Trey remarked. "And if you want my opinion, I would say that you are very lucky that the doctor back in Soda Lake did nothing for Tad except prescribe a purgative."

"A useless purgative."

An acrimonious look came over the gambler's face. "If it was just useless, that wouldn't be so bad. In Tad's case, the doctor's purgative may even have been harmful. I strongly recommend that you throw the bottle away."

"I already did," Kate admitted.

Trey smiled. "That's good."

"You've been most kind to look after Tad as you have, Mr. Wentworth. And I would like to thank you."

"Please, we have shared so much of this journey now. Don't you think you could call me Trey?"

Kate laughed. "If I call you Trey, the next thing you know, Tad will be calling you Trey."

Trey laughed with her. "Well, that wouldn't be so bad, would it? He seems to be a very bright and well-mannered boy—someone I wouldn't mind knowing." He paused and looked down at her. "As a matter of fact," he continued, his voice tender, "I don't mind admitting to you that I would like to know his mother better."

Kate's face was filled with surprise. She looked away, clearly nonplussed.

"I'm sorry. I didn't mean to make you uncomfortable," Trey said softly.

Looking back at him, she gave him a small smile. "That's all right. The truth is, I guess I'd like to know you better, as well. You're a most interesting person."

"You know what I mean, Kate," Trey said quietly.

For a long moment Kate and Trey looked at each other. Without thinking, the gambler reached out and stroked Kate's hair, telling her, "Your hair is so beautiful. I've noticed that when the sun strikes it, it almost looks as though it's on fire." He smiled knowingly. "It seems most appropriate, because I get the feeling you're a fiery woman, Kate Langston."

She laughed, and he instinctively leaned toward her until their lips were but inches apart. His hand moved to her shoulder, then to the back of her neck, and he felt her soft, warm skin. Putting his arms around her, Trey gently urged Kate's body against his. He bent his head, and for a brief moment their lips touched.

Then Kate suddenly pulled away and stepped back, and the gambler inwardly sighed. He knew that the beautiful woman standing an arm's length away from him had been longing for him as much as he had been longing for her, and he was startled by the depth of his feelings for her. It had been many years since he had allowed himself to be close to a woman in anything more than a purely physical way—no one, in fact since Christine—and he wondered if there had been anyone in the interval since Kate's husband had died.

She was staring at him, and he could almost feel the struggle within her. The attraction between them was powerful, and he was sure that she felt the same degree of desire for him as he was feeling for her. "Kate…" he whispered, his voice hoarse.

Kate shook her head and then looked around to make sure no one had seen them. "We…we shouldn't have done that."

He wondered how much of her hesitation was because he was a gambler—which was not exactly the most respectable of professions, after all. And he also found himself wondering whether, if he were to alter his way of living, she would find him suitable.

Trey was about to speak when Hank Bailey suddenly called from the other side of the stage, "All right, folks! Let's get back on the coach. We've got about five miles to go before we make camp for the night."

I may surprise you, Kate Langston, Trey Wentworth said to himself as he helped the beautiful redhead back into the coach. *And I may surprise myself as well.*

———

On a trail alongside the Powder River, on the opposite side of the mountains from the mining road, Brody Pike and his men awaited the stagecoach. It had been scheduled to pass by about two hours before sunset, and though it was not as yet completely dark, the sun had been down for almost an hour, and the stage had still not shown.

Rafe Dempsey walked over to a yucca plant and began to relieve himself.

"Hey, just what the hell do you think you're doin' there, Dempsey? Floodin' the valley?" Jim Porter asked to the amusement of the others.

"Nah, he's just waterin' the lilies, that's all," Jasper Maddox quipped, and again the comment was greeted with laughter.

Finishing, Dempsey buttoned his pants and turned toward the others. "Seems to me like you could think of somethin' more serious to be concerned with than me answerin' a call of nature," he grumbled.

"Like what?"

"Well, like where the hell is the stage?" he asked. "We been hangin' aroun' here practically all day."

"It'll be here," Pike said.

"That's what you been sayin' for hours," Dempsey

complained. "Hell, there ain't no stage comin' through this way. If there was, it would've been here by now."

"Maybe Dempsey's right. Maybe the stage ain't gonna come," Slim Hawkins remarked.

Brody Pike spat into the dust and then growled, "If it's come every other time, what makes you think it won't come this time?"

"Well, maybe we shouldn't have killed them people back at the way station," Dempsey suggested.

"What did you want to do? Leave them alive so they could warn the stage that we're here?" Pike asked.

"What I'm sayin' is maybe we done just that anyhow," Dempsey suggested. "If they got there and seen everybody dead, don't you think they got a mite suspicious?"

Pike ran a nervous hand through his lank hair. "I don't know," he admitted. "All right," he finally said. "I'll tell you what. Let's go back along the trail and see if we can maybe find out what's happened to them."

"How far back do you think we ought to go?" Dempsey asked.

"If need be, we'll ride all the way back to the way station."

"I don't know, Pike. You really want to go there?" Slim asked. "I mean, we left three dead men there."

"So we left three dead men there. So what? They wasn't no problem to handle when they was alive, what makes you worry about 'em now that they're dead?"

"It ain't that. It's just that…well, what if there's someone there askin' questions?" Slim queried.

"If they ask the wrong questions, we'll kill 'em," Pike said simply. "But I aim to find out what's happened to that damned stagecoach."

———

The travelers went another five miles, and the stagecoach once again rolled to a halt. Up top, Hank Bailey pointed to a grassy area between the road and a fast-running stream and said, "The place I picked out to camp is just down at the bottom of this here hill." He then scratched his beard, adding, "Only thing was, I never figured on it bein' this hard to get to."

Hank, Dingo, Clay, and Seth were looking at the obstacle that lay between them and what was to be their camp. About three hundred yards down the hill from the coach, the road suddenly curved to the right and then narrowed to what looked to be an impassable degree.

Setting the brake on the stage, Hank and Dingo walked down to look at the area. They stayed down there for a long time, talking and gesturing, and finally Seth, Clay, and Trey walked down to join them.

Seth asked Hank the question that was on everyone's mind. "What do you think? Can we make it through here all right?"

"Not any way that I can figure," the driver answered. "In fact, unless there's another route through here that I don't know about, we're just about stumped." Turning to Clay, Hank queried, "How about you? You know any other way through these mountains other than this here road?"

"No, I don't," Clay replied glumly. Folding his arms across his chest, he studied the roadbed and then said, "I've been here before, Hank, but I swear I don't remember the road being this narrow."

"Could be some of it got washed out," Dingo suggested. "Some of the rains in these here mountains are real gully washers. If the road ain't bein' used real regular, why it can start crumblin' away without anyone knowin' nothin' about it."

"I guess it don't matter if that's the case or not, 'cause it looks like we got no choice but to turn around and go back," Hank declared.

"Wait a minute," Trey put in. "Are you saying now that we should double back and then go up the other side of this mountain range, as originally planned?"

"I don't see any other way to do it than that way," Hank confirmed, shrugging.

"If we go back the other way, how long will that delay us in reaching Buffalo?" the gambler asked.

"It would add a whole day, I'm sure. Maybe a day and a half," Hank answered.

Trey shook his head. "Gentlemen, we can't do that. If we add one more day to the schedule, that boy back there is going to die."

"Now, hold on here, fella! Where do you get off saying something like that?" Hank asked. "You can't be sure about that."

"I'm afraid I am."

"What makes you so sure?" the driver asked, his voice mocking. "Is it your gambling instinct?'

"No, Mr. Bailey," Trey replied solemnly. "Unfortunately, this isn't a gamble. Take my word for it. If we don't get to Buffalo in a reasonable length of time, that boy is going to die. I haven't said anything to his mother, because I don't want to alarm her, but I am absolutely certain that Tad has an inflamed appendix —and if it ruptures, he will die. He may, of course, die anyway, even under a doctor's care, but if we could get him to Buffalo and a competent medical practitioner, he would at least have a fighting chance."

"Now, dammit, mister, you can't just come right out and make a statement like that…like maybe you're the high and mighty, or something," Hank said, exasperated. "You don't know for sure that that boy's goin' to die."

"Hank," Seth Reardon said quietly. "For what it's worth, I agree with Mr. Wentworth. I don't know anything about rupturing appendixes or anything like that, so I can't say that that is what is troubling the boy. But in my time I've seen death on a lot of faces— and I'm seein' it on that boy's face now. And if you think about it, you'll have to admit that you see it there, too."

"Damn!" Hank swore and then sighed. "All right. All right. Maybe I just didn't want to see it," he confessed. "All right, we'll go through. I don't even know how we're going to get the stage to the bottom of the hill—and if we do make it to the bottom of this one, who's to say we won't find another one just as bad tomorrow? But somehow we'll get this coach through, all the way to Buffalo."

"Maybe we ought to just camp at the top of the hill for the night," Dingo suggested. "Then we can figure out a way to tackle this road first thing in the morning."

"No, we may as well go ahead and try and get the stage down tonight," Hank countered. "It ain't gonna be no easier tomorrow."

Trey Wentworth studied the problematic section of road. A sheer rock wall about ten feet high bordered the right side of the road, while on the left there was a sharp drop of twenty to thirty feet. Dingo measured how wide it was from the wall to the drop-off, finding it was almost exactly the same width as the distance between the wheels of the coach. There was a variance of perhaps as little as three inches between staying on the road and dropping the outside wheel rims over the edge. Adding that the curve of the road, it meant that as the coach went downhill, it would also have to be turned within that tolerance of three inches.

"You know, if that coach tumbles over the side and takes the team with it, we're going to lose the horses," Hank remarked as he studied the situation. "Then we'd be set afoot out here. I mean, we could probably haul the damn coach back up, but it wouldn't do us no good with a dead or injured team."

"Yeah, that's true," the lawman agreed.

"Why don't we disconnect all the horses but one?" Dingo suggested. "That way we'd only be riskin' that one."

"Good thinking, Dingo," Clay said. "But maybe we could use two. One in front of the coach, and another connected by a rope to the rear. That way the horse at the rear could be used to hold the coach back as it starts down the hill."

Myron Haskell suddenly wandered down the hill and joined the other men. Looking smug, he declared, "Well, it looks like I was right after all, doesn't it? You have no choice now but to go back to the junction of Powder Creek and Willow Creek, then head up the other side of the mountain where there is a *decent* road."

"We aren't going back," Hank said. "We're going ahead."

"What? You plan to go ahead through here? Why, that's preposterous!" Haskell sputtered. "It's more than preposterous, it's…it's insane! And it is impossible!"

"Thanks for your opinion, Mr. Haskell," Hank snickered. He then looked at the others, asking, "Does anybody have any good ideas?"

"I think I know how we can do it," Trey suggested quietly.

"You!" Haskell hooted. "Oh, that's a good one. First you play doctor, now you are going to play stage driver. Tell me, Mr. Wentworth, just what makes you think you can drive a stage?"

"Oh, I don't think I can drive it," Trey replied. "It takes quite a bit of skill to handle a team and coach like this, and I know absolutely nothing about driving a stage. But I do understand mathematics and geometry. And that is the key that can get us out of here…if you would be interested in hearing it, Hank."

The driver threw up his hands. "Since I got no ideas of my own, I'd be more than willing to listen to what you got."

"What?" Haskell shouted. "Are you actually going

to give credence to this gambler? This is absolutely unbelievable! Turn the coach around! Turn around, I say, and take us up to the other side of the mountains as you were supposed to. I'll not risk this money and my life in some crazy scheme concocted by a gambler!"

"Mr. Haskell, I told you before and I'll tell you again," Hank Bailey said evenly. "We ain't holdin' you prisoner. If you don't want to ride along with the rest of us on this here coach, why, you're free to get off right here and right now."

Haskell looked around at the distant hills and mountains, vast and empty of any suggestion of civilization other than their own tiny pocket of humanity. "I'd be a fool to start out on my own out here," he retorted. "I've no idea where I am or which way to go. It would be suicide."

"Then you got no choice but to go along with the rest of us," Hank said. "And if you can't say nothin' to help us out, then, damn your hide, don't you say nothin' at all!"

"I'll remember that, Bailey!" Haskell snapped, pointing his finger at the driver. "I'll remember every word of it!"

"Oh, I'm sure you will, Mr. Haskell. I'm sure you will." Shaking his head, he turned to Wentworth. "All right, what's this here mathematical idea of yours?"

"Let me show you." Trey kneeled on the ground and then drew a semicircle in the dirt. "Let's say that this arc represents the segment of the road that we now occupy. If we were to carry the arc all the way through, we would have a circle—like so." He demonstrated his point by drawing a complete circle. "Now, all we have to do is determine the distance from the arc to the center of this circle. That would be the radius. If we anchored a rope at the radius and tied the other end onto the stage, we could more or less swing the coach around the arc. Even if the outer wheels slipped over the edge, it wouldn't matter, for the rope would keep it on its natural arc."

"I'll be damned," Hank said, grinning broadly. "You know, you just may have somethin' there!" He chuckled and then admitted, "I don't understand half of them words you was sayin' but lookin' at that plan of yours, I can tell that it's gonna work."

Standing, the gambler suggested, "If you gentlemen will tie the rope securely to the coach, I'll pace out enough of the road to determine the circle's radius. That way we'll know exactly how long the rope has to be and where to anchor it." He looked at the craggy wall lining one side of the road and added, "It shouldn't be too difficult to find the perfect boulder to use as the anchor."

"Then let's do it," Seth suggested, and he, Dingo, and Hank started back up to the coach to secure the rope, while Trey began pacing off the road. Periodically he would stop and use his pocket watch to measure the angles he needed to determine the radius.

As soon as the calculations were complete, the plan was put into operation. To the satisfaction and amazement of everyone, the coach, securely anchored by the radius rope, swung around the road as easily as if it were a giant pendulum. At one point, one of the rear wheels slipped over the edge, but the rope held the coach firmly in place, and it was a simple matter to guide the wheel back onto the road to continue.

Whooping with glee, Hank exclaimed, "That there experiment almost makes a body want to go back to school and get more learnin'!"

They began making camp, and the shotgunner remarked to everyone, "I tell you what. I can see why that feller's so good at poker. He's about the smartest feller I ever run across."

After a fire had been started, Seth Reardon stood and shouldered a rifle, saying, "We'll split up the watch during the night. Who wants the second one?"

"I have no intention of standing watch," Myron Haskell complained huffily.

"Mr. Haskell," Seth responded, "I have no intention of asking you. I want someone who is dependable."

The men agreed among themselves who would stand watch in what order. With that decided, the rest of the passengers settled down for the night.

Trey Wentworth walked over to where Kate Langston was sitting beside her son, who was sleeping fitfully. Kneeling beside her, he said softly, "How is he?"

"Not very well, I'm afraid," she answered, shaking her head slowly.

"Kate, I hope I didn't offend you earlier. I certainly wouldn't want to do that."

She put her hand on his arm. "It's all right. You don't have to apologize. I wasn't offended." She looked into his dark eyes and gave him a small smile. "Truthfully, Trey, you may very well be the most desirable man I have ever known. But I am a responsible, grown woman. I have a child to raise and a hotel to run—though a gambler moving from town to town, and getting run out of many of them, can't possibly understand that kind of responsibility." She sighed, adding, "At any rate, easy as I admit it would be to be swept off my feet by you, I can't afford to give my heart to a gambler. And especially not now. My only concern at this moment is for my son."

He nodded slowly. "I understand. And I want to help in any way I can."

Tilting her head, she studied him for a long moment, then said, "I do believe you mean that."

"I do. And as a matter of fact, I intend to make good on that promise. I'll go get some water from the stream. A cold compress on Tad's forehead may help bring his fever down somewhat."

Before Kate could respond, Trey stood and grabbed the water bucket that sat nearby and then hurried off.

———

Several miles south of where they had waited, Brody Pike and his men reached the Willow River junction. There, by the light of the full moon, they saw the tracks made by the coach and realized why it had not shown up when it was supposed to.

"Will you look at this?" Pike shouted angrily. "They went up the west side of the mountains! Now why do you suppose they did that?"

"Probably 'cause somehow they got wind that

we're after them," Dempsey said, his voice filled with scorn.

Ignoring the jibe, Pike smiled broadly. "Well, what do you know? They probably thought they fooled us good. Like as not they're halfway up the valley now, drinkin' coffee and celebratin' how they put one over on old Brody Pike. That's good, that's good. They'll think they've won now, so they won't be none too alert." He snorted and then added, "Get ready, fellas. We're gonna come down on them like a duck on a June bug."

EIGHT

S weeping over the travelers' campsite, the cool night breeze was so slight that the nearby trees did no more than whisper with its passing, but it felt pleasant against Clay Donovan's skin as he stood watch. In the distance, a coyote barked and then was answered by the long plaintive howl of another. Overhead, white stars blazed bright, seeming big and close.

Clay got up and tossed a chunk of wood onto the campfire. The fire was kept low so as not to be too visible, but Seth had decided they would be able to keep a low-burning fire, because they were down in a valley ringed by mountains. To see the fire, the observer would have to be on top of one of the surrounding mountains, though if the flames burned too brightly, its reflection could be seen from quite a distance, even from as far as another mountain range.

After watching the fire for a few moments to make certain it did not flare up, Clay then decided to walk to the stream. He passed the team where they were tied, and in the darkness, they appeared to be moving shadows within shadows. Standing by the edge of the stream, he looked across and into the trees.

Clay's mind drifted back to the conversation he had had earlier with Rebecca McBride, when he learned that the love he felt for her was not merely one-sided. If he understood what she was saying to him, and he believed he did, she loved him, too. And she had been just as confused—and had felt just as guilty—as he had because of it.

Clay was sure that Rebecca had never given Vince the least reason to doubt her love, even though she had loved Clay instead. Now, although Vince was dead and buried, he continued to come between them because the guilt Rebecca had felt for loving her fiancé's brother was just as strong as it had been when Vince was alive. Clay told himself that if he were honest with himself, he would admit that he felt a bit of guilt as well.

A scuffling sound interrupted Clay's thoughts, and he turned, his gun held at the ready. The tall, solid form of Seth Reardon was coming toward him.

"I saw you leave the camp and come down here," the lawman said. "Is everything all right?"

"Yes. I just felt like stretching my legs a bit," Clay answered.

Seth stroked his chin and looked back toward the encampment. "What do you think, Clay? Will Brody Pike hit us tonight?"

"I don't know," Clay admitted. "I have no doubt that he'll hit us during our trip—if not tonight, then certainly at some point before we reach Buffalo. He knows about the money, and he's damn well not about to let it get away from him."

"If he does hit us, it should prove to be a very interesting experience," Seth remarked wryly.

"Interesting? How do you mean?" Clay asked, regarding the lawman curiously. "That's a rather strange way of putting it."

Shrugging, the sheriff declared, "What I mean is, we've got ourselves quite a traveling circus here, wouldn't you say? Look at this group. We have a widow, a spoiled young girl, a sick little boy, a dude gambler, a jackass banker, a crusty stage driver— who's about ready to strangle the banker—a sawed-off shotgun guard, and you...an escaped prisoner."

"You left yourself out, Sheriff."

"Ah, yes," Seth responded, his tone ironic. "Well, I am the prize among us all. I am the sheriff, the one responsible for the protection of our little band, and I..." He paused for a long moment before he drew a deep breath and went on, "I am a coward."

"A coward? How can you say such a thing? You won the Medal of Honor—and unless I am sorely mistaken, the Medal of Honor isn't given for cowardice."

"Oh, yes, there is the medal, isn't there?" Seth mused, sighing. Folding his arms across his chest, he noted, "Well, let's just start with that, shall we? That medal has marked me ever since...*branding* me a hero, when the truth is, awarding it to me was the biggest joke the Army has ever pulled."

"You mean you didn't earn it? You weren't on that water detail?"

"Oh, yes, I was a member of the water detail. I did go down to the creek with the other men that day… Reno's Creek they call it now, though I imagine a few thousand Sioux have their own name for it. And like the others on the detail, I carried a dozen empty canteens, and I filled them with water."

"But that was dangerous, wasn't it?" Clay asked. "You aren't saying that no one on that detail deserved the medal, are you?"

"Oh, it was dangerous all right, and every man on that detail faced the danger bravely. You see, the Indians knew we would be needing water, and they were watching the stream closely. But getting down to the water and coming back alive was a matter of survival, that's all." He was silent for a long moment before continuing, "What the citation doesn't speak of is what I did earlier, when we crossed the stream to attack the village."

"What did you do?"

"I tucked my tail between my legs and I ran," Seth admitted. Squatting by the stream, he plunged his cupped hands in the water and scooped some up. He drank a little, splashed some on his face and then stood up and pulled a handkerchief from his pocket and wiped his face and hands before he continued the story.

"Seth, you don't have to tell me this," Clay said softly.

Shaking his head, Seth replied, "Clay, I've never told this story to a living soul, and it's haunted me ever since that June afternoon thirteen years ago. Now I want to tell it. I *need* to tell it."

Clay nodded. "I understand."

"I was a sergeant, attached to Major Reno's command," the lawman explained. "We received the order to attack the lower end of the village, and Custer was going to attack the upper end. The idea was to sweep through the village and meet in the middle."

"I take it that was before you knew how many Indians there were?"

"Oh, Custer knew, all right," Seth growled. "He just didn't give a damn. He thought he was invincible and could whip the whole Sioux Nation. I guess we did, too, because we started out in grand style. We crossed the river at a gallop and then charged toward the Indian village." Snorting derisively, Seth said mockingly, "Did I say village? It was a city, with every man, woman, and child armed and sworn to kill us. Halfway through our charge we realized that we weren't attacking, we were being attacked! Mounted and heavily armed Indians, five or six times our number, were coming toward us!

"We headed into a nearby gulley, and there Reno gave us the order to dismount. *Dismount!* I couldn't believe my ears! We were cavalry troopers, trained to fight from the saddle. Besides, when we dismounted, one in four had to hold the horses, so we immediately decreased our fighting force by twenty-five percent."

Clay kept silent as the lawman went on. "Reno was confused, and he kept giving contradictory orders. The officers and scouts around him were trying to convince him to remount and withdraw. One of the scouts was Bloody Knife, our most dependable—and my personal friend. Suddenly a bullet hit Bloody Knife in the face. It was a big one, either a huge ball fired from an old fowling piece or a fifty-caliber slug from something like a Sharps buffalo gun. Bloody Knife's head simply exploded—and blood and bone and brain matter splattered all over my face."

Unconsciously, Seth wiped his face with the handkerchief he was holding. "I didn't wait for any further commands. I jumped on my horse and started back for the river. A few seconds later, I heard Reno give the order to retreat, and the others came after me. I was the first one across the river and the first one to find a hole in the bluffs on the other side. But the funny thing is *no one knew I had run!* I had panicked, Clay, like a greenhorn private under fire for the first time...and nobody realized it, because the order for retreat came immediately afterward."

The big lawman looked down at his hands. "Later, when I learned I was going to be given a medal for getting the water, I tried to tell them I didn't deserve it. They thought I was just being modest, because I couldn't tell them what I had done at the gulley. I took the medal, under what to me were false pretenses, and when my enlistment was up, I got out of the Army."

The two men were quiet for a few seconds. Then Clay broke the silence, asking, "Seth, the order to retreat came almost immediately after you started to run, didn't it?"

"Yes, it did."

"Then you might say that the difference between running and retreating was a matter of rank."

"What do you mean?"

"You said yourself that Reno was confused and giving conflicting orders. Well, when he finally got his senses back, he ordered a retreat—something you already knew was necessary. If you had been a major and Reno a sergeant, then what you did wouldn't have been the running of a coward, it would have been the strategic withdrawal of a military commander."

Seth was lost in thought for a moment. Then he abruptly squeezed Clay's shoulder with a strong hand. "Maybe you're right," he said, a small smile on his face. "I guess I never thought of it quite like that before. Thanks." Stretching, he declared, "Well, I guess maybe I ought to go back up there and try and get a little sleep. My watch is at midnight."

He started for the camp and then stopped and looked back at Clay. "I hope some way we're able to prove your innocence, son. But if we can't, I'm going to have to send you back to prison."

"I hope it doesn't come to that, Seth," Clay replied. "Because I'm not going back."

"Are you saying you would fight me?" the lawman asked.

"If need be," the young prisoner confessed with a nod.

The sheriff smiled thinly and then drew an audible breath. "Well, my friend, if it does reach the point that there's a showdown between us, I guess we'll learn once and for all, won't we?"

"Learn what?"

"Whether my action at Little Bighorn was the

running of a coward or the strategic withdrawal of a
military commander."

———

Rebecca McBride was restlessly shifting on her blanket
near the fire when she saw Seth Reardon come back
into the camp, then lie down. Within a few moments
Seth Reardon was snoring contentedly, as were all the
others. The young woman envied them, for they had
been able to fall asleep quickly, whereas she was still
trying to find a position that was comfortable.

She turned over for what had to be the hundredth
time and stared out toward the creek bank. She could
make out Clay Donovan standing there, illuminated
by the full moon, sometimes looking all around the
horizon and other times just staring at the water. She
wondered what he was thinking about. More specifi-
cally, she wondered if he was thinking about her.

Rebecca continued to toss and turn, but no matter
how hard she tried, sleep refused to come. Finally she
sat up and watched the campfire for a few moments,
then she decided to take a little walk. She assumed she
would be safe as long as she stayed well within sight
and sound of the encampment.

She noiselessly made her way down to the creek
bank, most of her way lighted by the glow of the small
campfire, stopping upstream somewhat from Clay and
unseen by him. Walking to the edge of the water, she
watched the rushing water, splashing a brilliant white
where it broke over the rocks.

The air caressed her skin like fine silk, carrying on

it a hint of wood smoke and coffee. She suddenly wondered whether anyone was near; if so, they would be able to smell the encampment even if they could not see the flames from the fire. Putting the thought from her mind as she pulled her shawl tighter around her shoulders, she looked around as her eyes adjusted to the darkness.

The night sky looked like blue velvet, and the stars glistened like diamonds, while in the distance, barely visible mountain peaks rose in great and mysterious dark slabs against the midnight sky. An owl landed nearby and his wings made a soft whir as he flew by.

If Rebecca still had any doubts about abandoning her original intention to return to Boston, this night put them to rest. Despite the dangers they were facing —or, though she could scarcely admit this to herself, because of them—she had never felt so alive.

Glancing to her right, she saw a large, flat rock, and she walked over and sat. Pulling her knees up under her chin, she stared out at the water, and the constant gurgling of the brook soothed her while she sat in contemplative silence.

She thought back a few hours, when she and Kate Langston had sat talking by the fire. The two women had discussed Trey Wentworth, and Rebecca was sure she had detected something in Kate that had not been there earlier in the day. There was a sparkle in her eyes when she spoke of Trey, but when Rebecca questioned her about it, Kate had insisted it was merely that she was so touched by the gambler's compassion—not something one would expect to find in someone of his profession.

Rebecca, on the other hand, was more impressed with Trey's wealth of knowledge about music, literature, and art—subjects she would never have expected a gambler to understand, much less know. She prided herself on her fine Boston education, yet the two of them had wiled away many of the hours during the long journey discussing the works of various artists, writers, and composers, and it had been clear that the gambler not only knew his subjects well, but he held interesting opinions on them. It had also been clear to her that Trey's background was not that of the rough-and-tumble wanderer, and she was very sure that he was much deeper than he appeared to be.

"It's not a good idea for you to wander away from the camp like this," a voice suddenly declared. "Though I'll confess I'm glad you did."

Rebecca had been so absorbed in her own thoughts that she had neither seen nor heard Clay Donovan approach her. Nevertheless, she was not surprised by his presence. "Aren't you supposed to be on watch?" she asked offhandedly, without looking up from the water.

"I *am* on watch, which explains why I'm here," Clay replied dryly. "What about you?"

"I couldn't sleep."

"You've been traveling hard ever since you left Boston," he observed. "I can't imagine you not being tired enough to sleep."

"Maybe I just have too much on my mind."

He sighed. "I can understand that. I have a lot on my mind, too." His voice softened. "I hope some of it is the same thing."

She still would not look at him. "Clay, what's going to happen to you?"

"What do you mean?"

"As much as I disagree with that awful Mr. Haskell, he is right about one thing. You're an escaped prisoner. When we arrive in Buffalo, you'll be sent back to the penitentiary."

"Yeah, that's what Seth Reardon just reminded me," Clay remarked. "But I'll tell you what I told him. I'm not going back."

"How are you going to arrange that?"

"There is no doubt in my mind that Brody Pike is going to attack the stagecoach somewhere between here and Buffalo. The money we're carrying is as much bait to him as cheese is to a rat. And when he takes the bait, I'm going to take that two-legged rat."

"I see. So your entire plan is based upon capturing Brody Pike and somehow forcing him to clear you, is that it?"

"That's it," Clay agreed.

"What if it doesn't work out that way?" Rebecca asked. "What if you aren't able to capture him?"

"Then I'll figure out some other way. No matter what it takes, Rebecca, I am not going back to prison."

"Even if it means running from the law for the rest of your life?"

"Yes," Clay answered. "If it comes to that, then I'm prepared to do just that."

"That certainly wouldn't be much of a life," she suggested.

"No, it wouldn't be." Clay reached down and put his hand under her chin and then gently turned her face up to look into his own. "That's why I could never ask you to come with me. Before a man would ask a woman to marry him, he should have something to offer her...a home, security, and a future."

She felt her face coloring. "Marriage?" she asked, the work catching in her throat.

"Yes," he whispered. "I love you, Rebecca McBride. I have always loved you, and I always will."

"Oh, Clay," Rebecca said. She was about to protest that such feelings were inappropriate, that she could not reciprocate his desire to marry, but before she could say anything further, Clay lifted her to her feet and pressed his lips against hers.

A tidal wave of pleasure washed over Rebecca, and despite all her resolve not to act upon her feelings for him, despite her carefully reasoned logic for staying clear of him, she found herself dissolving under the fire of his kiss. As the intensity of his kiss grew, she pressed her body against his, feeling heat coursing through her as if she had turned to molten metal.

Finally Clay pulled away from her. "Rebecca," he began, his voice forceful, "I love you, and I want to know how you feel about me."

The young woman sighed. "I love you, Clay," she confessed in a small voice.

Clay turned away from her then and put his hand to his forehead. "Damn!" he exclaimed.

She gasped in surprise. "What is it? I tell you I love you, and you act as though I've slapped you in the face."

He looked back at her, a bittersweet smile on his lips. "Don't you see it, girl? Now that we can finally tell each other how we really feel, there's nothing we can do about it—unless I can prove my innocence."

"Well, then," Rebecca said resolutely, stepping to him and putting her hands on his shoulders, "we shall just have to prove your innocence. Now that I've admitted my love, I don't intend to let you get away from me."

Clay smiled broadly and pulled her to him again, folding her into his arms in a bear hug. "That's all I need to hear," he murmured into her ear. "Rebecca, I'm going to get Brody Pike and make him tell what actually happened that day. If I have to soak my pants in kerosene and ride down to hell to kick the devil in the backside to do it, it's going to be done."

Rebecca laughed. "Well. Clay Donovan, I suppose if you insist on doing that, the least I can do is hold the kerosene can for you."

"Deal!" he exclaimed and then sealed their bargain with another kiss.

———

"The trail goes that way," Brody Pike insisted, pointing toward the mountains.

"No, it don't. It goes that way, through that pass," Rafe Dempsey replied, pointing in a different direction.

"Dammit, I once held up a mule train over here. I know where the trail is."

"Were they pack mules, or were they pullin' a wagon?"

Pike looked at his man in bewilderment. "Pack mules," he answered.

"Well, there you go," Dempsey said. "Pack mules can use a mountain trail. A wagon needs a road—and the road goes through that pass."

"The moon's gone down, and it's too dark to make out much from the sign," Slim Hawkins interjected. "Maybe we ought to wait until light and then get a bean on them. I mean, if we strike out down one of these two trails you're arguin' about, and we choose the wrong one, we might lose 'em."

"All right, all right," Pike agreed reluctantly. "We'll stay here till dawn." He pulled off a plug of chewing tobacco and stuck it in his cheek. Scowling, he grumbled, "We're supposed to have a friend on the coach. Why in hell don't we get some kind of a signal?"

———

Dingo poked at the dying fire with a long stick until the coals that had been glowing broke out into flames. He then tossed a few more chunks of wood onto the fire, and when he was satisfied that they had caught, he sat down on a rock and watched them burn.

His gaze fell on Myron Haskell some thirty feet away from him. The clerk lay sleeping with his arms wrapped securely around the black bag he had carried ever since he had boarded the coach in Medicine Bow. And in that bag was one hundred thousand dollars.

Dingo tried to imagine what one hundred thousand dollars looked like—and how long it would take to spend it. The most money he had ever had at one time was six hundred and thirty dollars—the money he had stolen from the Kansas Stage Line. He had proceeded to lose most of it in a poker game just two days later, and the rest he had spent on women, whiskey, and food.

Dingo smiled. The whiskey had been rotgut, and the whores had been ugly, but the food had been wonderful. After he had been caught and sent to prison, he used to pass the long hours by thinking back on some of the food he had enjoyed during that little spree: steaks, chops, roast beef, and—which he discovered to his great surprise that he liked—mutton. The law had caught up with him as he was leaving a restaurant in Abilene, but the timing had been perfect. He had just spent his last dime.

Thinking about the money in Haskell's satchel, the shotgunner smiled again. With that much money—or even a share of it—he could leave the territory and maybe go out to San Francisco or even back east, to someplace like Boston. The law would never think of looking for him back east.

He had heard the beautiful McBride girl talk about what a wonderful place Boston was, and he wondered how many restaurants Boston had—and how long it would take someone to eat his way through all of them. With enough money, it would probably take a long time…

———

Seth Reardon was not sure what caused him to wake up, but he abruptly opened his eyes and lay there for a moment, feeling as if something was wrong. Glancing over toward the stagecoach, he saw that it appeared to be all right as it stood clearly illuminated by the bright orange flames from the campfire. Suddenly he realized that the coach would not be as plain to see as it was unless the campfire was too big. Leaping to his feet, he looked over and saw that the fire was blazing brightly, providing a beacon that could lead anyone—including Brody Pike and his men—right into the camp.

"What the hell!" Seth bellowed. "Who's on watch here? Who built up this fire?"

Clay Donovan sat up on his blanket and sleepily replied, "Dingo. Dingo's supposed to be on watch."

Dingo had been sound asleep, slumped forward against a log, but the sudden shout woke him.

"Get that fire down!" Seth ordered as he rushed to contain the blaze.

Dingo leaped up and began kicking dirt onto the flames with the sheriff. Brought under control, the fire was once again a small glow rather than a huge blaze.

"Dingo, what the hell were you trying to do? Were you sending a signal to Pike and his men?" the lawman challenged.

"Sheriff, I swear to you, I don't know how that fire got so big," Dingo countered. "I mean, it's true I fell asleep, and there was no excuse for that. But there wasn't enough wood on the fire to allow it to build to such a blaze. I swear it!"

"Then how do you account for the fact that it was just that? Wood doesn't just jump into a fire."

"I admit it looks suspicious," Dingo said, "but I didn't do it."

Shaking his head, a look of skepticism on his face, the lawman muttered, "It'll take more'n just your say-so to convince me, I'm afraid."

The others were all awake now, and Seth Reardon turned away from Dingo and addressed everyone else. "All right, folks, as long as we're all up, we may as well break camp. It'll be light soon, and we need to get underway."

Everyone began stirring, rolling up blankets and packing away cooking gear. The women walked down to the stream and splashed water on their faces and then combed their hair.

As they returned to the others, Kate Langston remarked to Rebecca McBride, "I'll be awfully glad when we reach Buffalo and I'll be able to wash my hair. I feel as though there's a peck of trail dust covering it." She gave the young brunette a sidelong glance, adding, "I must say that I'm surprise you're taking our hardships so lightly."

Rebecca blushed and looked down at her feet. "Yes, well, I guess perhaps I've discovered that there's more Wyoming than Massachusetts in me after all."

Kate cocked her head and studied Rebecca for a long moment but said nothing. She then walked over to where her son lay on the ground and gathered him into her arms, carrying him over to the stagecoach.

Hurrying to help Kate carry Tad into the coach, Trey Wentworth was sure that the boy was steadily growing worse. He had checked him as soon as they had been awakened and discovered that the child's fever had increased during the night, as had his pain. As the others busied themselves with loading everything back on the stagecoach, Trey took a bucket and walked down to the stream. There he broke off chunks of the ice that had formed along the edges and filled the bucket with it. By the time he returned to the stage, the team was hitched and the passengers were boarding.

As the coach got under way, the gambler took out his pocketknife and cut a bit of canvas from the window curtain and then began wrapping it around a large chunk of ice. Clay looked at him as if he had lost his mind.

"Trey, what are you doing?" he asked, bewilderment written on his face.

"When I get finished with this, it's going to be a most serviceable ice pack. And I'm going to have Mrs. Langston hold this on Tad's stomach, right about there." He pointed to the lower right side of the boy's abdomen.

Kate looked at him with a questioning expression on her own face. "That seems like a rather strange thing to do," she said. "Tad's in so much discomfort as it is, why would I wish to increase it?"

"Because it'll accomplish two things," the gambler answered. "It'll numb his abdomen so that the pain won't be quite as severe, and it'll slow the infection." He sighed and then told her, "I haven't wanted to alarm you, but I'm convinced he has appendicitis."

"Appendi...what?" Kate responded.

"Appendicitis. The appendix is swollen and

inflamed. Hopefully the cold will keep it from bursting before we reach Buffalo, but if it does burst, it might help retard the spread of the infection until your Dr. Colburn can perform an appendectomy—that is, remove the appendix. It's a surgical procedure."

"Oh, my god!" Kate exclaimed, putting her hand to her mouth in fright. "That'll be very dangerous, won't it?"

"There's a degree of risk, yes, but it isn't nearly as dangerous as letting the appendix rupture." Trey handed the canvas-covered ice to Kate. "Here, put this on him," he instructed.

Kate laid the ice pack on Tad's stomach, but Tad instantly jumped and cried out in pain. "Oh, Mama, don't! That's so cold, it hurts!"

Kate jerked her hand away, but Trey reached across the space between the seats and put his hand on her wrist. Gently, but firmly, he guided the ice pack back on Tad's stomach. "Keep it there," he ordered. "It will be uncomfortable only briefly, and then he won't feel the cold anymore—nor, hopefully, the pain."

"All right," Kate agreed, although her expression clearly bespoke her uncertainty. She held the ice pack in place, despite the complaints and whimpers of the boy.

"Madam, for the life of me, I can't understand why you insist upon doing everything this man tell you," Myron Haskell said.

"Well, I think she should listen to him," Clay put in. "I don't know anything about doctoring, but it seems to me like most of it is just common sense—and

I've never known anybody with more common sense than this man. You saw how he managed to get us down the mountain last night."

"Yes, I saw. It was a damn fool stunt that could've gotten us all killed," Haskell sputtered.

"It was a very smart feat," Clay corrected, his blue eyes flashing. "I wouldn't call it a stunt at all."

There were murmurs of agreement from the other passengers. Then Trey turned to Kate and looked her intently in the eyes. "I don't mean to force you to do anything you don't want to do."

"Nonsense, I trust you," Kate responded.

I trust you! The words were like a dagger in Trey Wentworth's heart, for they were the same words uttered by Christine before he operated on her...before he *killed* her.

For a moment, Trey almost told Kate Langston to take the ice pack away. After all, who was he to give advice? He had walked away from the responsibility of his Hippocratic oath. He was no longer a doctor— not in the eyes of the world and certainly not in his own eyes. But just as he was about to say something, Tad spoke.

"Mr. Wentworth was right, Mama. I don't feel it anymore, and my stomach's quit hurting."

"There, that's excellent," the gambler said, sighing with relief that the numbing had taken effect so quickly.

Kate put her free hand on Trey's. "How can I ever thank you for what you've done for my son? I owe you a great deal."

Putting his other hand over hers, Trey remarked,

"Nonsense. You don't owe me a thing. I'm glad I was able to help you, Kate—you and Tad both. I'd like to get to know him better, after all."

The two of them looked at each other for a long moment. Then Kate blushed and pulled her hand from Trey's. Obviously embarrassed, Kate glanced at each of the other passengers, but the only one who was watching her was Rebecca McBride, and she had a conspiratorial smile on her face.

———

The stagecoach had been traveling for about a half hour when Clay Donovan stared more intently out the window. Something had caught the corner of his eye, and as he looked, he saw it again. It was a patch of reflected light, playing along the rocks. Puzzled, he leaned out the window and looked up and then saw that it was Dingo's rifle, flashing in the sun.

"Hold it! Hold it!" he shouted.

"Whoa!" Hank Bailey called to the team, and with a squeak of brakes, the coach came to a halt.

Clay flung open the door and leaped out, standing with his hands on his hips and staring up at the box.

"What is it?" Seth Reardon asked from his position atop the stage.

"It's Dingo's rifle," Clay answered. "Look over there on the rocks."

Seth, Hank, and Dingo looked in the direction that Clay indicated. Then the shotgun guard jiggled the rifle in his grip, and the patch of light danced around before them.

"Dammit, Dingo, what the hell are you doing?" Hank asked.

"Get that rifle wrapped in something, Dingo!" Seth ordered. "The way that thing's flashing, someone could see us for twenty miles."

"Hell, I'm sorry!" Dingo yelped, reaching quickly for his duster. "I'll keep a watch on it. It won't happen again."

"It better not," the lawman snapped. "First there was the fire, now this. What's next? Smoke signals?"

They got back on the road, with Clay keeping an eye peeled out the window. Not ten minutes passed when a rifle shot abruptly rang out, followed by the whine of bullets.

"Clay!" Seth shouted from atop the coach. "They're here! They're behind us!"

"Move over, Seth, I'm coming up top!" Clay shouted back. As he threw open the door, he looked at the other passengers and instructed, "Pike and his men'll be shooting high—at us. Trey, put the boy and the women on the floor, and you and Haskell lie down in the seats."

"I can shoot as well, you know," Trey yelled over the gunshots coming from up top.

"Are you any good?"

"Not very."

Clay shook his head. "Then don't bother. If they see that shooting's coming from down in the coach, they'll shoot back. Let us handle it."

Reaching for the luggage rack, Clay pulled himself up on top of the stage. By now Hank had whipped the horses into a dead run, and the coach was bouncing and lurching at full speed along the little-used wagon road. Dingo had left his place in the driver's box and positioned himself on the coach top with the sheriff. Joining the others, who lay as flat as they could and still take aim, Clay began shooting back at the attackers.

A bullet whizzed by Clay's ear, and he immediately flattened himself against the coach top.

"How many are there?" Clay shouted at Seth.

"I've seen five!" the lawman yelled.

"Yeah, that's what was at his camp!" Clay confirmed.

The wheels of the coach were throwing up dust, which made it difficult to see clearly enough to get a good shot. But it made it just as difficult for Brody Pike and his men to see the defenders.

Clay Donovan got to his knees to take aim when suddenly the coach hit a deep wagon rut, and he was thrown off balance. He found himself hanging over the side of the luggage rack, his face precariously close to the wheel. Grabbing desperately for something to hold on to, his hand found the sidelight, and he gripped it with all his might while dust and rocks were thrown up into his face. Closing his eyes, he found that made the sensation even worse. Then a bullet fired by one of Pike's men zinged close to his head, and he instinctively ducked.

"Hang on, Clay!" Seth shouted. "We'll get you up!"

While Dingo kept up the shooting, the muscular lawman hurried to Clay's aid. Clay felt himself being lifted up by the seat of his pants and hauled to safely.

"Whew, boy!" Seth shouted. "Don't do that again!"

Clay grinned. "I'll try not to!" he promised.

Repositioning themselves, Clay and Seth resumed the defense.

Dingo fired, and Clay saw one of Pike's men grab his right knee as blood poured through his pant leg. Then Seth got off a good shot, and another one of the gang grabbed his stomach and then tumbled backward off his horse.

Suddenly Brody Pike called to his men, "Fall back! Fall back!" The robbers then abruptly all reined in their horses while the stagecoach continued on ahead.

"We did it!" Seth Reardon shouted triumphantly.

"Yeah," Clay responded, "but for how long?"

———

"Dammit, Pike, they're gettin' away!" Rafe Dempsey said.

"And with our money," Slim Hawkins added.

"Just hold on, boys," Pike responded, looking at his men. Slim and Dempsey were uninjured, but Jim Porter was white as a sheet from the pain of his shattered kneecap, and his right leg was covered with blood from the knee down. Jasper Maddox was lying face down and unmoving in the dirt about a quarter of a mile back, and Pike was sure he was dead.

"What'd we stop for?" Dempsey asked.

"There's too many of them bastards for us to take 'em this way," Pike told him. "Who'd have thought they'd have that many guns?"

"Well, you ain't gonna let the money get away, are you?"

"Naw," Pike replied, a slow smile working its way over his hard face. "Don't forget, we got us a friend on that coach. I figure if we'll just hang back a bit, he'll get it stopped for us." He chuckled, adding, "Why work so hard when we don't have to?"

NINE

"Hank! Hold it up, Hank!" Dingo shouted forward to the driver. "Pike and his bunch have pulled back! You can stop the team now!"

Looking back over his shoulder, Hank Bailey verified that the outlaws had withdrawn. "Whoa, horses!" he yelled, hauling back on the reins, and pushing the brake lever forward with his foot. The stage squeaked and rattled to a halt, sitting on the lumber road surrounded by a cloud of dirt and dust that had been thrown up by the gallop. Completely exhausted by their effort and their bodies covered with foam and sweat, the horses stood shuddering in their harness with their chests heaving and breathing loudly.

"My god, listen to those poor critters," Hank declared in a pained voice. His weathered face wore a worried look as he continued, "Damn me if it doesn't just kill my soul to do this to 'em." Then he smiled, asking, "Weren't they magnificent, though? They gave us all they had—and this after they'd pulled us for two days before I put them to this runnin'. But they're plumb wore out now. If I don't give 'em a short rest, they're gonna drop dead in their traces, every last one of 'em."

"Go ahead and give them a rest," Seth Reardon agreed, shifting around on the top of the stagecoach so that he was facing forward. "I think Brody Pike's had enough. I don't think we'll be seein' anything else from him. Not now, anyway." He grinned and then remarked, "After all, we kinda narrowed his odds."

"I wouldn't be giving up on him just yet, Seth," Clay Donovan cautioned, wiping a forearm across his thick sandy hair to keep the sweat from running down into his eyes. "Maybe he won't hit us head on, but you'd be making a big mistake if you believe he's given up. I can't see Brody Pike just walking away from all this money without attempting another try."

"Well, don't worry, I'm not going to let my guard down, if that's what you mean. But I think we hurt him pretty bad, and I figure ol' Pike is going to have to lick his wounds for a bit. He needs this time about as much as we need it to let our horses blow."

"I'll admit that we probably bought ourselves a little time," Clay said. "You might even say we won the battle...though the war isn't over yet." He lay his rifle down. "If you don't mind, Sheriff, I'm going to hop down and have a look at the folks inside the coach. Pike and his boys threw a lot of lead at us. I want to make sure nobody got hit by a stray bullet."

"Yeah, that's a good idea. Especially the boy. I'm mighty worried about that little tyke."

"Yeah, me, too." Clay dropped down to the ground and then opened the door and looked inside.

"Any bullets come through here?" he asked, looking directly at Rebecca McBride, his eyes filled with concern.

"No bullets. Just dirt," Rebecca answered as she ran her hands over her face.

"Yeah, I guess I can see that," Clay said dryly.

The passengers in the coach looked as if they had all been wallowing like hogs, for they were coated with the same thin film of gray-brown that now covered the stage—dirt and dust that had been thrown up by the hooves and wheels during the mad dash just completed. Myron Haskell, drawn up in the front left corner of the coach, was clutching a handkerchief to his nose.

"I guess it got a little rough for you folks, but we couldn't help it. Is everybody all right?" Clay asked.

"No, we are not all right!" Haskell replied testily, his fingers smoothing his small, clipped mustache. "That fool driver nearly broke our necks with that wild ride he just gave us!"

"You're still alive, aren't you, mister?" Clay snapped.

"Barely."

"Well, barely's better'n dead. You should be thankful. Believe me, you wouldn't even be that if Pike had caught up with us."

"I disagree. In fact, I think we should stop and wait for Pike to come to us," Haskell said.

"What? You think we should stop and wait for

him? What's the matter with you, mister? Are you crazy?" Clay asked, dumbfounded.

"Not in the least. In fact, I believe myself to be the only sane person around here. Perhaps if we stop the coach and approach Pike under a flag of truce, we could negotiate with him."

"Negotiate? Negotiate for what?" Clay asked, his voice rising.

"Why, negotiate for our lives, of course," Haskell replied. "I have some degree of experience in business negotiations...I am a banker, after all. I would be more than glad to represent our side in this matter. I know that the only thing Pike wants is the money. If we simply give it to him, I'm sure he would ride away and leave us alone. I don't believe he would kill us without any reason."

"Those men we buried back at the Powder River way station might disagree with you, Mr. Haskell," Clay retorted. "And anyway, you're the one carrying the money, so that means you're the one Brody Pike and his gang are after. I would think you'd appreciate our fighting them off more than anyone."

"Yes, well, whereas I am carrying the money, it is, after all, the Medicine Bow Bank's money and not mine," Haskell corrected.

Clay ran an impatient hand through his dust-colored hair. "It may be the bank's money, but you do have some responsibility for it."

"I have some responsibility, of course, but I think we have made an adequate attempt to defend it," the fussy little clerk countered. "We have fought well, and there would be no dishonor in surrendering to Pike's demands. Indeed, I know of no code of honor that would require us to die for one hundred thousand dollars of someone else's money."

"No, Mr. Haskell, I don't reckon you would know of such a code of honor," Clay barked. "But then, what difference would it make? I'm not sure someone like you would abide by any such rules anyway."

"Sir! Are you accusing me of being a man without honesty?" Haskell demanded.

"No. Just a man without honor," Clay replied. "And in my book, you can't have one without the other."

He looked over at Kate Langston then, dismissing the unpleasant Myron Haskell. Kate was holding Tad's head on her lap, Rebecca was holding the boy's feet, while Trey Wentworth was kneeling between the seats, with his hand resting on Tad's stomach.

"The sheriff wants to know how the boy's doing," Clay asked. "And I'd like to know myself." Studying Tad, Clay was not at all reassured by the child's appearance. His face was very pale, and it was obvious that he was hurting badly.

"The ride we just took didn't help things much," Trey replied.

"I'm sorry about the ride, there was nothing—"

The gambler held up his hand, cutting off Clay's apology. "No, no, don't start apologizing. I know it couldn't be helped. I was just making an observation, I wasn't complaining." He pulled Tad's shirt back down and then took his seat, looking across at Kate.

"How is he?" she asked anxiously.

"There's no doubt that the boy is in a great deal of

discomfort," the gambler replied. Then he smiled. "However, from everything I can determine, any pain he's feeling now is from the banging around of the rough ride. I'm almost positive that his appendix hasn't burst."

"Good," Kate breathed. Then she tilted her head and stared intently at Trey. "I mean, I think that's good, isn't it?"

"Oh, yes," he assured her. "That's good." He reached down in the bucket and pulled out another chunk of ice. "I sure do wish we had some more ice though," he said as he wrapped the small chunk in the canvas. "I'm afraid this is our last piece." He handed it across to Kate.

Just then Seth Reardon climbed down from the top of the coach and stood beside Clay, looking in through the doorway.

"No damages in here," Clay reported.

"Good," the sheriff declared. "Come on, son. Let's hike back along the road a piece and see if we can get an idea as to where Pike might be."

"All right," Clay agreed, and the two men started walking.

"How's the boy doing?" Seth asked.

"Well, according to Trey, whatever it is that's ailing the boy hasn't burst, and that's supposed to be a good sign," Clay answered. Then he shook his head, adding, "But he's in a lot of pain."

"Poor kid," Seth said, sighing. "I wish we could just give him a nice, smooth ride on in to the doctor." His clear blue eyes turned cold. "It really makes me furious, Pike putting a child through all this."

"Brody Pike never has been known as a compassionate man," Clay observed. "It makes no difference to him whether he's dealing with a man, woman, or child—everyone is treated equally brutally."

When they were far enough away from the coach to ensure that they could not be overheard, then Seth and Clay turned and looked back at the others. Hank was up at the front of the team, examining his horses, and Dingo was leaning nonchalantly against the side of the coach, cradling his rifle in his arms. Haskell was the only passenger who had left the coach, and he was walking around nervously, stretching his legs.

Looking back at Clay, the sheriff told him, "I want to talk to you about Dingo."

"Dingo? What about him?"

"Turns out, Dingo served a prison sentence some time ago in Kansas. And it was for robbing a stagecoach."

"How do you know this?"

"Soon after he started working for the Wyoming Express Company, I found an old wanted poster on him," Seth explained. "Naturally, I checked up on him, but I learned that he wasn't wanted anymore. He had served his time and got a full release."

"I see. Did you tell the stagecoach people?"

"No," Seth replied, shaking his head. Then he sighed. "I know, I know, I probably should have. But I sort of like Dingo, cantankerous old sort that he is, and I figured he had already paid society whatever debt he owed. If he was trying to make an honest living now, I didn't want to do anything that would cause him problems. Besides, I figure since the stagecoach company never asked anything about him, it wasn't my place to volunteer any information."

Bending, Clay picked up a rock and started tossing it from hand to hand. "How has he worked out?"

"Pretty well. From all I hear, Dingo's been one of their best employees—at least, he has been till now. Tell me, Clay, do you think he's in cahoots with Pike? I mean, first there was the business with the fire last night, then there was the flashing rifle coming just before Pike attacked us…"

"I don't know," Clay answered. Then he admitted, "Actually, I knew he was in prison. And as a matter of fact, he was Pike's cellmate."

"He was?" Seth punched his fist into his hand. "Then damn it, that settles it! He's got to be our man!"

"Maybe. But I saw one of Pike's men go down with a shot-out kneecap, and I'm pretty sure it was Dingo who got him."

"Well, what if Dingo shot him on purpose? You know, to make it look like he's on the level. He didn't kill the man, after all." Scratching his head, ruffling his gray hair, the lawman added, "By the way, how'd you know he and Pike shared the same cell?"

"He told me," Clay replied. "And that's another reason I don't think he's guilty. If he were in on this, why would he tell me Pike was his cellmate?"

"I don't know. Maybe it's because you're a fellow convict," Seth reasoned. "Maybe he just trusts you not to tell."

"Perhaps," the young prisoner acknowledged with a frown.

Seth started to speak but then hesitated. Finally he

asked, "Clay...if he said he'd cut you in on part of the money if you'd keep quiet, you'd let me know wouldn't you?"

Scowling, Clay threw the rock hard against a tree. Turning to the lawman, he then responded, "Seth, come on, I thought you knew me better than to ask a question like that. Are you still not completely convinced that my brother and I are innocent?"

"Oh, I believe you were innocent all right, but you've been serving time for it anyway—and I think it's human nature to want to get even. You may figure you're owed some of the money that's on this stage."

"If you really believe that, why are you letting me carry a gun?"

"Because I *don't* really believe it, I guess," Seth admitted with a sigh. "Hell, I'm not supposed to be on this stage anyway. If my horse hadn't gone lame, I'd already be back in Buffalo, wondering what was taking the stage so long to get there."

Clay smiled. "Well then, aren't you glad you're here with us so you can have your curiosity satisfied?"

Laughing, the lawman replied, "You know, they say curiosity once killed a cat. I just hope that doesn't hold true for sheriffs."

Suddenly Hank Bailey's voice rode the air. "Seth! Clay! The horses have got their breath back. I think we can leave if you two are of a mind!"

"Be right there, Hank," Seth shouted back, and he and Clay turned and started toward the coach. Looking at his prisoner, the sheriff had a wry grin on his face as he remarked, "You know, I sort of hope Pike does try again. If he does, we'll burn him good." He then chuckled, adding, "Only I want you to promise to leave the fella in the top hat to me. I've never shot anyone as elegantly dressed as that."

Clay laughed, promising, "He's all yours."

They reached the coach, and everyone re-boarded, with Seth Reardon and Clay Donovan once again riding on top, their weapons held at the ready. But the vehicle had gotten no farther than a half mile when the left rear wheel suddenly seized up.

"Whoa!" Hank called to his team, hauling back on the reins again.

"What now?" Seth asked.

"If it's not one thing, it's another," Hank said, tying off the reins. "Something's wrong with one of the wheels. One of the ones in the rear, I think. Feels like it's locked up tighter'n a drum."

Hank climbed down from the coach while everyone watched with concern. Checking the wheels, he found the troublesome one and put his hand on the hub. Hank then removed some of the axle grease and rubbed it between his fingers.

"I'll be damned," he breathed.

"What is it?" Seth asked from up top.

Holding his grease-stained fingers out toward the lawman, Hank answered, "This is full of grit. Someone's put dirt in the hub." Narrowing his eyes, he observed unnecessarily, "One of us on this here stage don't want us to get through."

"But...who would do such a thing?" Rebecca McBride, her head sticking out the window, asked in a disbelieving voice.

"I'll tell you who it is!" Myron Haskell said,

climbing out of the stage and brushing himself off. "It's him!" He pointed an accusing finger up at Clay. "I warned all of you! I told you not to let an outlaw ride with us! Now look what he has done!"

"Haskell, we don't know that he did it," Seth insisted.

"Well, I know he did it, whether any of the rest of you want to admit it or not," the clerk declared, his voice self-righteous.

"Right now it don't make no difference who done it," Hank Bailey grumbled. "The thing we gotta do is get that wheel off and get all the dirty grease out of there. Then I can goop her down good with some clean grease, and we can reset the wheel and get going."

"How long is all that going to take?" Trey Wentworth asked, sticking his head out the window.

"Not too long, if we'll just get on it," the driver answered.

Pointing up to a shadowed, snow-covered ledge some fifty feet up the side of the mountain that bordered the road, Trey noted, "We've run out of ice for the boy's stomach. Will I have time to climb up there and get some snow?"

Hank looked up at the snowbank and then nodded. "Sure, I reckon you'll have time to do that."

"Good." He looked across at Kate Langston and told her, "Don't worry. We'll keep him comfortable."

"Thank you, Trey," she murmured, her gratitude obvious.

The gambler hopped off the stage, and the driver poked his head inside. "I'm gonna have to ask you folks to get out. Sorry about havin' to disturb the boy, but it can't be helped."

"Of course," Kate responded, helping Tad to his feet. The woman and the boy then climbed off the stage.

Glancing around, Hank shook his head and observed, "Even with the jack, it's gonna take at least three of us to get this stage lifted. Sheriff, it you and Clay'll help Dingo get her raised up, I'll pull the wheel." He smiled ruefully. "I'm afraid this here jack don't do nothin' to make our job easier. All's it does is provide a base to rest the axle on once we get 'er raised." Turning to the bank clerk, he then suggested, "Mr. Haskell, you and the ladies can keep a sharp lookout for Brody Pike and his bunch."

Tad shuffled over to the opposite side of the road, where he found a place to lie down. With the boy safely out of the way, Kate, Rebecca, and Haskell took up their posts to act as lookouts.

The men began working. It proved to be hard, heavy labor, and they were well into it, sweating and shoving to make sure the coach was lifted and the jack put into position.

Suddenly Tad called out, "Mama! Come quick! I'm hurting real bad!"

Kate's head whipped around. She then looked back at Rebecca and Haskell and told them in a shaky voice, "I have to go to him."

Rebecca watched her hurry off, and Haskell offered, "Miss McBride, you can go help her if you want. I'll keep watch."

Clearly surprised by her fellow traveler's uncharacteristically generous offer, the young woman responded, "Oh, thank you, Mr. Haskell, I appreciate it." Then she lifted her long skirt and hurried over to Kate and her son.

For the next few minutes, all were involved in what they were doing. The women tried to soothe the boy, while the four men grunted and groaned as they hurried to complete their job. Then suddenly an evil laugh rang out, and a loud, gruff voice taunted, "Well, now, lookee here, would you?"

Everyone turned to see Brody Pike holding a pistol pointed at them. Two other men were with Pike, one wearing a Mexican serape and the other wearing dirty formal striped trousers and a top hat. They, like their leader, had revolvers trained on the travelers.

"Pike!" Clay growled.

"That's right," the outlaw confirmed dryly. Then his cadaverous face hardened, and he snarled, "Now, how about you fellas unhooking your holsters and letting your guns drop?" When Dingo started inching toward his shotgun, Pike aimed his pistol directly at him and warned, "Try it, Dingo, and you're a dead man. Maybe I should'a slit your throat five years ago instead of givin' you that nice souvenir you're wearin'. You sure did cause me a peck of trouble after rattin' on me."

Fingering his scar, Dingo looked at the outlaw with loathing. "You didn't have to kill that kid in the pen. All's he did was try to protect his property."

Smirking, Pike agreed, "That's true. But I wanted it, and that's all that mattered." He then glared at

Dingo and said, "And all that matters now is that you obey me."

The shotgun guard said nothing more and moved back.

"Ah, that's more like it." Looking over at Clay, Pike cautioned, "And you, fella, you seem a mite slow in droppin' your gun. I'd get rid of it now, if I was you. And kick it out of reach."

With a slow sigh of frustration, Clay pulled his pistol out, using thumb and forefinger on the butt, and dropped it in the dirt and kicked it aside.

"Now you're bein' smart," Pike mocked.

"Yeah, but I guess I wasn't smart enough two years ago," Clay rejoined coldly. "I let you get the better of me then."

Pike squinted his eyes and studied his adversary for a moment. "Say, I know you, don't I?"

"In a manner of speaking," came the bitter reply. "My name's Clay Donovan. Does that mean anything to you?"

Laughing gleefully, the outlaw answered, "Well, I'll be damned! Yeah, I know who you are now. You went to prison for that bank job up in Banner."

"I went to prison, but I didn't pull the job—as you well know."

Pike's dark piercing eyes narrowed. "I didn't know you was out."

"How could you? But I paid your camp a visit the other night."

A broad smile slowly spread over the outlaw's gaunt face, and he exclaimed, "So, that was you! I've been wonderin' who that was pokin' around out there in the dark. Tell me, Donovan, I thought you was supposed to be in prison for—what was it?—twenty years. How'd you get out of jail, anyway?"

"I broke out."

"Is that a fact? Well, ain't that a hell of a thing." He looked over at the two men with him. "Well now, boys, what do you think about that? Our friend here broke out of prison. Maybe we should take him into our gang. We need a good man now, what with these fellas killin' Maddox and bustin' up Porter's knee so bad we had to leave him back there in the hills. What do you say, Donovan? You want to join up?"

"No, thanks," Clay answered. "I have other plans in mind. Matter of fact, I've been looking forward to meeting you for a long time."

"I'll bet you have," Pike responded with a laugh. "But right now, I'm more interested in the money. Where's it at?"

"It's in the coach," Myron Haskell spoke up. "I'll get it for you."

Haskell opened the door to the stagecoach and took out the satchel, and then he opened the bag and reached inside. "You'll find it all here. I've put it in packets of one thousand dollars each."

"Just throw the whole thing over here, Banker," Pike ordered.

Haskell drew himself up to his full five feet three inches. "I most certainly will not!" he replied indignantly. "I will give you exactly fifty thousand dollars, which is your share. Fifty thousand and no more. And I trust you brought me a horse."

Turning to his men, Pike began mimicking Haskell.

"I trust you brought me a horse." He laughed uproariously, and his cohorts laughed with him. Then he turned back to face Haskell, and the smile left his face. "There's somethin' you don't understand, Banker. It's *all* my share," he said coldly.

"Now, just you wait a minute!" Haskell shouted. "Who set this up? I did! I told you about the money, I built up the fire last night to guide you to us when we left the trail, and I sabotaged the stage so it would have to—"

That was as far as Haskell got, because Pike raised his revolver and shot him without so much as blinking an eye.

"What? No…" Myron Haskell gasped, clutching his chest, and looking down in surprise as blood spilled through his fingers. "You cheated me…you cheated—" He took a step toward Pike and then pitched forward and fell face down in the dirt.

"Troublesome little bastard, wasn't he?" the gang leader said.

"Mr. Haskell!" Rebecca McBride screamed as she raced to the clerk. Kneeling beside him, she put her hand on his neck.

"Ain't no need in checkin' on him, Missy. He was dead by the time he hit the ground," the outlaw remarked.

Rebecca looked up at the outlaw with her eyes blazing fire. "Do you think you're going to get away with shooting him down in cold blood like that?" she asked angrily. "We all saw you do it!"

"Yeah, and I thought you'd be happy to see him go first," the outlaw said. "After all, he's the one who got you into this mess. But it don't matter none. You're all gonna have to die." He looked at her appraisingly. "Too bad about you though, honey. You sure are a looker."

"Pike, answer one question for me first, will you?" Clay Donovan suddenly asked.

"Sure, why not?"

"When you killed my brother two years ago and framed me for the bank robbery, why didn't you kill me, too?"

"What good would that have done?" Pike replied, amusement in his eyes. "If I'd killed both of you, the posse wouldn't have even slowed down. By me leavin' you alive like that, that dumb marshal figured he was on to somethin', so he forgot all about me and my boys so he could take you back for a big trial."

"Then he *was* telling the truth?" Seth Reardon asked. "He was innocent all along?"

Pike laughed. "As innocent as a newborn babe. Or" —he added with a chuckle—"you might say a lamb being led to the slaughter."

"Thank you, Pike," Clay put in. "You've just cleared me."

"Yeah? Well, it's too bad you won't be alive to enjoy it."

Nodding slowly, Clay then asked the outlaw how he had arranged the deal with Haskell. He had no interest in knowing the answer, it was merely a ploy to keep the man talking, playing for time, because unseen by Pike and his men, Trey Wentworth was slipping quietly down the side of the mountain from where he had gone for snow. Finally halting about ten feet above and behind the outlaws, Trey's right hand held the revolver he normally carried in his holster, while in his left was the derringer that he carried hidden up his sleeve.

Then he turned the pistol around so that he was holding it by the barrel. He made a tiny pitching motion with his hand, and Clay nodded almost imperceptibly that he understood.

"Turn around, Pike!" the gambler suddenly shouted. At the same time, Trey tossed the revolver through the air toward Clay.

Startled by the unexpected voice, Pike and his men turned abruptly, their weapons aimed high. Trey fired his derringer, then dove behind a rock. Although he was out of range for such a weapon, it was not important that he hit anything just that he provide a diversion.

Brody Pike, Rafe Dempsey, and Slim Hawkins all immediately fired back at the gambler, despite the fact that he was well protected.

"Pike!" Clay shouted.

Pike spun back around and it was evident that he was shocked to see the revolver in Clay's hand. The two men fired simultaneously, but while Pike's bullet slammed harmlessly into the side of the coach, Clay's slug found its mark. The outlaw leader clutched his throat, and blood spurted between his fingers. A startled look on his face, he stared wordlessly at his enemy and then sank to his knees. He coughed once and then crumpled to the ground, his eyes staring vacantly.

In the meantime, Seth, Hank, and Dingo managed to recover their own weapons, and a gun battle erupted. With the opening shots, Kate and Rebecca threw themselves on the ground, covering Tad's body with their own. The little valley echoed with the sounds of gunfire, and bullets whistled off the rocks.

With no time for anyone to leap for cover, the men shot it out at near point-blank range. The two remaining outlaws were badly outnumbered. Disorganized, they shot wildly, barely coming close to their foes. Clay fired at the outlaw wearing the serape, leaving the one in the top hat—as promised—to Seth Reardon. He thought he had the man pinned down when suddenly a bullet whistled close to his ear. Swearing loudly, Clay aimed carefully and fired, and Slim Hawkins screamed in pain and then fell flat.

Seth then took out his quarry. After blowing a hole in Rafe Dempsey's top hat, whisking it off the man's head, the sheriff planted another slug right between the outlaw's eyes. Dempsey's fingers froze around the handle of his revolver as he sank to his knees and then flopped onto his back, staring sightlessly at the sky.

For a long moment, everyone stood rooted to the spot, as if in shock. The air hung heavy with the smell of spent gunpowder, and a billowing cloud of blue smoke drifted lazily away.

"Is everyone all right down there?" Trey Wentworth called, rising cautiously from behind the rock.

"Gambling Man," Seth Reardon shouted, holding on to his arm, which had sustained a flesh wound, "you got my word. You can stay in Buffalo as long as you want. No matter what kind of committee the folks may get up against you, I'll insist you'll always be welcome."

"If they go against him, they're going to have to go against me, too," Kate Langston added, smiling broadly.

"And I'll be standing right beside you, Kate," Rebecca McBride agreed.

Climbing down from the hillside, Trey suggested, "How about if we all save the praise for when we get back to Buffalo? And the sooner we get that wheel back on, the sooner we'll be there. Don't forget, we've got a sick boy on our hands."

Nodding, Hank Bailey said, "Right you are! All right, men, let's get to it."

As Clay stepped to the coach, he looked at Seth and asked, "What about that guy with the bullet through his knee? He's somewhere back on the trail."

Nodding, the lawman responded, "The way he was losing blood, he won't get far. As soon as we reach Buffalo, I'll send out a couple of men to go after him."

As soon as the wheel had been remounted, everyone re-boarded the stagecoach. With the threat of robbery no longer hanging over their heads, Clay Donovan and Seth Reardon were once again able to ride inside.

Just as Seth was about to step aboard, he looked up at Dingo and said, "By the way. There's something I've been meaning to ask you. I saw you go into the tele-graph office in Medicine Bow just before we departed, and I gotta confess that for a while there, I thought maybe you'd sent some kind of message to Pike. Now, I know it's none of my business to ask—"

"That's all right, Sheriff," Dingo cut in. "I ain't got

nothin' to hide. Fact is, Hank sent me over to get a message off to Miss McBride's papa. He promised he'd let Mr. McBride know that his daughter'd got in all right on the train and was headin' to home."

Smiling sheepishly, the lawman said, "I guess I could've saved myself a whole lot of wondering if I'd just asked you before."

Dingo grinned, and for a moment he looked closer to thirty-five than fifty. "Yeah," he agreed. "I guess you could have."

TEN

It was evident that Tad Langston's condition was worsening. His pain had increased, his fever was up, and his pulse rate was fast. Trey Wentworth never left the boy's side, keeping a steady watch over him.

He looked up at Kate, whose face was pale with fear, and his heart went out to her. Putting his hand over hers, he said softly, "He'll make it. I promise."

A tear trickled down Kate's cheek, and her lower lip trembled. "How can you be so sure?" she asked, her voice barely a whisper.

"I just am. Trust me."

She gave the gambler a small smile. "I do, you know. I really do."

He smiled back reassuringly and then once again put all his attention on the gravely ill child.

Whenever the road would allow it, Hank Bailey kept the horses going at a fast trot. They were coming down from the mountains now, and the road was a great deal better than it had been. As a result, they were able to make much better time than had been possible since leaving the main road.

Finally they rolled into Buffalo at twenty minutes before midnight, and Hank did not even bother to stop at the stage depot. Instead he urged the team into a gallop, and the coach rumbled down the main street until it reached Dr. Wesley Colburn's office.

The coach lurched to a halt, and Trey leaped down and ran to the physician's door. He pounded hard for a few moments and then lights came on inside. Several more moments passed, and then the door was flung open. An elderly man clad in a nightshirt stood in the doorway holding a kerosene lamp.

"Yes? What can I do for you?"

"I'm looking for Dr. Colburn."

"I am Dr. Colburn," the kindly looking white-haired man said, stepping out onto the porch.

"Thank God!" Trey breathed. "We have a critically ill child on board, Doctor. Have you a stretcher?"

"'Course I have a stretcher," the doctor replied, obviously surprised by the question. "This is a medical facility, you know."

Nodding, the gambler said, "I'm sorry, I didn't mean to imply..." His words trailed off, and he turned and hurried back to the stage.

"Come on, Dingo," Clay Donovan said. "Help me get the stretcher." Then he and the shotgun guard hurried into the doctor's office. A few minutes later they returned, carrying the stretcher between them.

Working carefully from inside, Trey and Seth Reardon lifted the boy from where he had been lying between his mother and Rebecca McBride and gently carried him to the doorway. Hank Bailey guided Tad onto the stretcher, and then Dingo and Clay carried the boy into the doctor's office and placed him on the examining table.

Everyone else had by then crowded inside.

"Doctor, the boy has appendicitis," Trey explained.

The physician smiled patronizingly at the man in black. "Why don't you just let me be the judge of that?" he replied. Looking Trey up and down, he added, "I'd say medical diagnoses are a bit out of your field, sir." As he started to examine Tad, he asked, "But just out of curiosity, what makes you think the child is suffering from appendicitis?"

"He has severe abdominal pain that started near the umbilicus, then localized in the lower right side. He has no appetite and has suffered from nausea and fever. His pulse has remained strong but is rapid."

The amused expression left Colburn's face and he looked at Trey in surprise. "You're right," he said. "Those *are* the symptoms of appendicitis."

"I stabilized the condition by the application of ice packs. It numbed him against the pain and kept the appendix from rupturing so far, but you're going to have to operate, Doctor. His appendix must come out."

"Let's not be so hasty."

"No, that's just it, Dr. Colburn. We must be hasty. This child has been suffering for days. We've waited as long as we can."

"Mister, I'm not sure you understand what you're saying," the physician said. "You're talking about abdominal invasive surgery." Colburn shook his head. "I can't do that. Why, it could kill the boy."

"There is some degree of danger, of course, but it can be greatly minimized if you do the procedure properly," Trey insisted.

"And I suppose you are going to tell me how to do it properly?"

"If you wish," the gambler answered, ignoring the mocking tone. "Make a transverse incision, then ligate the meso-appendix and remove it by the Paquelin cautery. Tie off the stump and cauterize it, then close him back up. But make certain that your hands and the instruments you use are absolutely clean. You must introduce nothing into the wound that could cause infection."

Kate Langston stood with her mouth open. Finally she asked, "Trey, who *are* you? You are obviously not just a gambler."

"I am now," he told her.

"And before now?"

Trey let out a long sigh. "I was a doctor," he admitted.

"What is your name?" Colburn asked.

"Wentworth."

"Wentworth…Wentworth… See here, you wouldn't be Caleb Wentworth, would you?"

"Yes. Caleb Alexander Wentworth. The third. That's where Trey comes from," he added to Kate.

"Well, I'll be damned," Colburn said. "Doctor, the whole world is wondering what happened to you."

Looking more confused than ever, Kate remarked, "Dr. Colburn, you've obviously heard of Trey."

"My dear, your friend here was one of the best surgeons in the country. Why, I read about him even out here." Turning to the gambler, he asked, "But what happened to you, Dr. Wentworth? You just dropped out of sight, as I recall."

"Look," Trey said. "We can discuss all this later. The most important thing now is to operate on the boy. If you don't get that appendix out soon, it's going to rupture. And if it ruptures, I don't have to tell you that the boy will probably die."

Shaking his head firmly, Colburn declared, "It's not that simple."

"If you wish, I will assist," Trey offered.

Colburn shook his head again. "You don't understand. I simply can't do it. I don't have the skills for such an operation. And even if I did, my hands just wouldn't cooperate." He held up his fingers, and Trey saw that they had been twisted and gnarled by arthritis.

"But you must have performed operations," Trey insisted.

"Oh, yes. I've set a few bones and extracted more than my share of bullets. I'm all right as a country doctor, handing out medicine and the like, but I can't handle a scalpel. No, Doctor, if this boy's appendix is going to come out, then *you* are the one who will have to take it out."

The gambler's face turned pale. "Me? No, absolutely not. The boy is your patient, not mine."

"Oh, Trey, you can do the operation, can't you?" Kate asked, wringing her hands and looking up at him pleadingly.

"Kate, you don't know what you're asking of me," Trey said.

"Oh, but I do know," Kate replied. "I'm asking you to save my son."

Trey started to object, but he quickly realized that there was no other option if the boy was to survive. His decision was forced when Tad clutched his side and cried out in agony. Bending over the boy, the gambler examined him and realized that the appendix was on the verge of rupturing.

He stood up, his face tortured. "Dammit!" he whispered. Closing his eyes, he pinched the bridge of his nose for a moment and then took a deep breath and let out a long and slow sigh. "All right," he finally relented. "All right, I'll do the operation."

"I'll assist," Colburn offered. "What instruments will you need?"

Trey told him and then asked, "Do you have any carbolic acid?"

"Yes, I do," the elderly physician replied.

"Would you please pour it into a tray and then empty my instruments into that tray?"

"Yes, of course, Doctor," Colburn replied.

Trey then started preparing Tad for the operation, washing him thoroughly and then administering chloroform to anesthetize him. He then scrubbed his own hands repeatedly and, with that done, returned to his patient.

Finally looking up from the youngster, Trey faced Kate Langston and suggested. "It would be best if you wait outside. Operations are very bloody, and I don't want you to worry at the sight of so much blood coming from your son."

Kate was clearly reluctant to leave her son, but she went into the anteroom, joining the others, who were all waiting anxiously.

Looking over his shoulder at the white-haired physician, Trey told him, "Doctor, I'm going to ask that you wash your hands as thoroughly as I just did."

While Colburn was following instructions, Trey stood over the boy. His heart was beating fast as he held his hands out in front of him, palms up. Though he had done many appendectomies in his career, always considering them simple operations, it had been a long time since he had last performed one. His confidence had been shattered by his fiancée's death, and now this boy and his mother were much more than an impersonal patient and family. They had become important to him—just as Christine had been important to him when he had operated on her tumor against the advice of his fellow surgeons.

He breathed a quick prayer; then, when Colburn joined him at the table and handed him the scalpel, Trey took it in hand and began.

Cutting into the abdomen, he bared the swollen appendix. He worked quickly and efficiently and began making the incisions and slicing through the tissue required to remove the diseased organ.

Suddenly the boy went into respiratory arrest. Trey felt his own heart begin pounding, and he cried, "No! Not again! I won't let this happen again!"

Working desperately, he pulled Tad out of the crisis and reestablished a steady heartbeat and respiration.

He was sweating profusely, and Dr. Colburn dabbed gauze on the surgeon's forehead, mopping it dry.

"That was close, son," Colburn breathed.

"Too close," Trey agreed.

The older man smiled. "But close doesn't count, after all."

Nodding, Trey admitted, "No, I suppose it doesn't, does it?"

Minutes after that, he removed the diseased organ and began closing up the wound. With the last suture finally in place, he sighed with relief and then put the bloodied scalpel back into the tray and walked wearily to the door of the surgery.

He leaned against the doorjamb for a moment, letting his heart slow down, and then pulled open the door.

Kate, who had been pacing anxiously, stopped short and then rushed to him. "How—?"

"He's going to be just fine," he cut in. "Tad's a strong little boy, and he's well on his way to recovery. There's nothing to worry about now."

With a shout of joy, Kate threw herself into Trey's arms.

———

A week later, Tad was released from the doctor's clinic, and Kate celebrated with a dinner in her newly reopened hotel. She invited everyone who had been on the stage, plus Dr. Colburn and Rebecca's father, Kevin, and Hank Bailey's wife and son.

It was an exceptionally happy dinner. Tad was

healthy again, as evidenced by the return of an appetite that let him eat two pieces of apple pie. Rebecca McBride's father, Kevin, was delighted to have his daughter home again. And Clay Donovan was celebrating the fact that he had just received official notification that the original court order that had sent him to prison had been reversed. Further, he had received a full pardon from the territorial governor for the prison break and stealing the visiting lawyer's horse, clothes, and gun.

"I suppose you'll be staying on out at your ranch," Kevin McBride remarked to Clay. "You'll be wanting to build it up again."

"I'd like to, yes, sir," Clay responded. "Of course, it's going to take me a while to get back to the point Vince and I had reached before he was killed and I was sent to prison, but I intend to do just that."

"Perhaps it won't take you as long as you think," Kevin suggested.

"Why? What do you mean?"

He smiled broadly. "Well, let's just say I like having good neighbors. What if I loaned you a hundred head of cattle, bulls, and cows, to get you started? Would you accept it?"

"Well, sure!" Clay exclaimed, a grin lighting up his handsome face. "That would be wonderful! I mean, that's much more than just being neighborly. Actually, I don't know how I could ever thank you, Mr. McBride."

Kevin chuckled. "Young man, consider it the act of a selfish parent. I don't want my daughter going back to Boston, and I figure having you around here might just keep her in Wyoming." He laughed, adding, "I have a feeling from the way you two look at each other that it's all going to be in the family anyway."

Clay's grin got even wider, and he reached over and took Rebecca's hand. "Mr. McBride, if I have anything to say about it, that's exactly the way it's going to be."

"Well," Dr. Colburn spoke up, "now that that's settled, I wonder if we could prevail upon Dr. Wentworth to stay here as well, I could use a young partner —and Wyoming could certainly use a good surgeon." He smiled at the younger physician and asked, "What do you say, Trey?"

"I don't know," Trey replied. He turned to Kate, gazed at her lovingly, and then asked, "What do you think? Does Wyoming need me?"

"I don't know about Wyoming," Kate answered, putting her hand over his, her brown eyes sparkling with pleasure. "But I sure do."

A LOOK AT

THE HUNT FOR BIG CAT

THERE WAS SILVER IN THE HILLS...AND BLOOD ON THE LAND.

Wyatt Langston, a burly stage driver with dreams of a better life, never expected his route through the lawless mining camps north of San Francisco to become a fight for survival. With bandits and bushwhackers lurking in every shadow, danger is part of the job. But it's the mysterious Ku Xuan, a half-Chinese beauty with secrets of her own, who's upending Wyatt's world.

On a quest to find her American father, known only as "Big Cat," Ku Xuan hides a deadly truth—she's a Shan Tal priestess, trained in the ancient martial arts of the Orient. Her life has been shadowed by assassins and those who would see her silenced forever.

Now, Wyatt and Ku find themselves caught in a deadly crossfire: a ruthless killer is seeking revenge on Wyatt, a master assassin from Ku's past is hunting her with lethal precision, and a sea captain long thought dead is returning to face his own demons—and he's ready to die for them.

In a land where greed and violence rule, Wyatt must fight not only for his life but for the woman who holds his heart as the line between survival and loyalty blurs in a storm of bullets and betrayal.

AVAILABLE NOW

ABOUT THE AUTHOR

Robert Vaughan sold his first book when he was nineteen. That was several years and nearly five-hundred books ago. Since then, he has written the novelization for the mini-series Andersonville, as well as wrote, produced, and appeared in the History Channel documentary Vietnam Homecoming.

Vaughan's books have hit the *NYT* bestseller list seven times. He has won the Spur Award, the Porgie Award in Best Paperback Original, the Western Fictioneers Lifetime Achievement Award, the Readwest President's Award for Excellence in Western Fiction, and is a member of the American Writers Hall of Fame and a Pulitzer Prize nominee.

He is also a retired army officer, helicopter pilot with three tours in Vietnam, who has received the Distinguished Flying Cross, the Purple Heart, The Bronze Star with three oak leaf clusters, the Air Medal for valor with 35 oak leaf clusters, the Army Commendation Medal, the Meritorious Service Medal, and the Vietnamese Cross of Gallantry.

Made in United States
Troutdale, OR
06/10/2025

32028285R00132